Nightshade

To: Melissa

With love,

Johnny [illegible]

Nightshade

Johnny Bullard
White Springs, Fla.

ISBN-10: 1518736637
ISBN-13: 978-1518736636

Printed in the United States of America

Acknowledgements

This book is dedicated to the memory of my father, Wade Bullard, who loved me unconditionally, as well as to my two best friends, Sue and Carolyn Burkett, who have always believed in me, and to my dear mother, who, through thick and thin, has never stopped loving me.

I offer a special thank you to my editor, cajoler, guide, dear friend, novelist, and one of the greatest reporters I've ever known, Joyce Marie Taylor, who helped me make this dream come true.

Many thanks go out to photographer John Stokes of Lake City, Florida for the breathtaking photo he allowed me to use on the cover.

From the Eight Mile Still on the Woodpecker Route north of White Springs, I wish you all a day filled with joy, peace, and above all, lots of love and laughter.

May God bless each and every one of you,

Johnny Bullard

Chapter 1

Wild coreopsis and pastel colored phlox were in full bloom along both sides of dusty, white sand roads in and around the small town of Seraph Springs in Campbell County. The intoxicating scent of honeysuckle penetrated the humid air as it meandered through the woods, around the trees, and along the fence lines.

Deep within the woods, in a sunlit clearing, another plant was growing wild, only this one was laced with poison, and in the wrong hands it could be deadly.

Scientifically known as Atropa belladonna, the Deadly Nightshade plant was widely used around the Middle Ages, both medicinally and cosmetically, but it was also used for evil intentions.

Deadly Nightshade is beautiful to gaze upon with its dark purple, bell-shaped flowers, tinged with a soft splatter of green around the edges. Its shiny, dark purplish-black berries have the power to entice the innocent to savor its sweet juices. Its slight fragrance can even trick the uneducated into thinking it is safe to touch and to consume.

The sun, with its golden splendor and warmth, seemed to welcome this time of year with open arms. It beamed down with benevolence upon the dark waters of the Suwannee River and upon the crystalline waters of the Blue Hole, a relatively small, spring-fed tributary of the river that many folks in the community utilized as their own personal swimming pool. The water was clear and icy cold, and the beach around the old swimming hole was banked like spun sugar.

Yes, summer had definitely arrived in all its glory and danger in this region of north central Florida.

Wanda Faye Easley and her sister, Nadine Lloyd, both sixth generation north Floridians, were lounging in dinosaur-shaped floats over at Blue Hole Spring, which was just west of the sleepy town of Seraph Springs where they both lived.

Wanda Faye started laughing uncontrollably while she was in the middle of gulping down her iced tea, which was in a large pink plastic cup.

"What's so funny?" Nadine asked, looking over at her sister, who now had tea spilling out of the cup all over her chin and down her neck.

"Did you see that old hippie gal come down

here a few minutes ago?" Wanda Faye asked her, still laughing. "I think her name was Moonbeam. I watched her fill them gallon jugs with this river water and then she toted 'em back up the hill. You could tell she didn't have on a bra or drawers underneath that flimsy dress."

"Yep, I seen her," Nadine said, laughing along with Wanda Faye now. "I also seen her underarms. My God! All that hair! You coulda' braided that stuff for hours, it was so long. God knows, there ain't none of them hippie gals ever won a beauty contest. Hell, there ain't none of them ever *been* in a beauty contest!"

This sent both girls into more fits of laughter. After she calmed down, Wanda Faye adjusted her oversized, white-rimmed sunglasses, which had slipped down off the bridge of her nose. Then, she motioned for Nadine to hand her the plastic sandwich bag she had hanging from around her neck with a piece of string. Today was her turn to carry the stash and make sure it didn't get wet.

Inside the plastic bag were two packs of cigarettes and two Bic lighters, a red one and a purple one. Both girls smoked the same brand, Marlboro Reds, so it was easy and convenient for them to loan cigarettes when one of them was running low.

Only thirteen months apart in age, the two of them looked at least seven to eight years older than their twenty-two and twenty-three years.

Part of the reason for the quicker than normal aging was the collective seven children they had between them, who were splashing in the little slough not ten feet away from where they were floating.

Wanda Faye had three boys and a girl; Chester Jr., who was nicknamed Little Chet, Victor Newman, because Wanda Faye loved the soap opera character on *The Young and the Restless*, John Lewis, named after the circuit judge and the county sheriff, with whom she was well acquainted, and her last little baby, Jewell Lee, who was named after Wanda Faye's mother, with Lee being her mother's maiden name.

Nadine had two girls, a set of twins; Charlene and Darlene, and one son, Dale Earnhardt, named for the famed race car driver.

This was a rare day of leisure for the two young mothers, as they were both off from the poultry processing plant where they worked the night shift. They had volunteered for the dreaded shift when they hired on, so they could be at home when their children got home from school. Between family, friends and neighbors in the tight-knit community of Seraph Springs, there was never a shortage of babysitters to watch the children while the two girls were at work.

Eight hours each night from ten until six in the morning, the two ladies plucked and dressed chickens for the grand sum of eight dollars and fifty cents an hour.

Wanda Faye's ex-husband, Chester Easley Sr., was serving the last year of his three-year sentence in the federal penitentiary in Georgia for selling drugs. Her divorce from him became final last year, thanks to the efforts of her dear friend, Carl Alvin Campbell.

Wanda Faye had wondered for a long time why she and the children were living in a government-subsidized apartment in Seraph Springs – along with most of the town's poor blacks and whites – if Chester was making so much money from manufacturing and selling crystal methamphetamines, which was what the court documents stated he was charged with. At this point, she figured it was a question that would never be answered.

After taking a deep drag from her cigarette, Wanda Faye sighed and said, "What I need is to dress up, go out to eat a good shrimp supper, have a couple of cold drinks, and spend an evening with someone tall, dark and handsome."

"Well, Sis," Nadine replied, as she nodded her head to the right. "Could be your opportunity is coming down the hill now."

Wanda Faye looked over to see Drayfuss Lowell, better known around town as Dink, walking down the hill carrying a small cooler. He was wearing a pair of cut-off blue jean shorts and a ratty looking T-shirt. She noticed he had gotten a little paunchy over the last several months, ever since his wife ran off with a deputy sheriff over in the next county, but he still had a fairly decent physique from what she could see in the distance.

According to his ex-wife, when they were still a loving couple, Dink was endowed like a young stud horse, which didn't exactly explain the nickname he'd been given, unless one was talking about opposites. The cut-off shorts he was wearing were slightly baggy, so if he was hung like a horse, it wasn't all that apparent to the casual onlooker. When he spotted the girls, he called out to them.

"Hey, Nadine! Wanda Fay!" he shouted. "Y'all got the youngun's in swimming today?"

"Oh, Lord, yes!" Nadine shouted back. "It's so hot you could fry an egg on the patio outside my trailer! That air conditioning costs so much, I just run it at night!"

"I know the feeling!" Dink yelled back.

He quickened his pace and started down the hill toward where the girls were floating out in the water.

"I had to come down here to cool off myself," Dink said, as he set down his cooler and a dingy, white beach towel on the edge of the shoreline. "Been workin' on them log trucks for my brothers all morning. Finally got to a stopping point. Pretended like I was runnin' to the parts house for a while, and here I am," he added with a sly grin.

"Well, aren't you the slick one?" Nadine teased him, but all Dink did was grin a little wider.

"You girls want a little pick-me-up in that iced tea? I know you got the babies and all, but I got a little vodka in my cooler. It's some of that lemon flavored stuff. Might taste pretty good in that sweet iced tea."

"Why, Dink, I always did say you was a gentleman," Wanda Faye said, turning on her feminine charm. "Yes, I'd love a little splash. Can't speak for my sister, but a little pick-me-up would do me just fine."

Dink reached into the cooler, took out a quart bottle of Fleischmann's that was nearly half empty, made sure no one nearby was watching him, and then he started over toward the girls. By this time, Nadine was holding out her cup, too.

While Dink was wading out to them, Wanda Faye noticed he was staring at her. With her dark, reflective sunglasses on, she knew he couldn't see her staring back. She also knew he was drooling over her well-endowed bosom. She was quite proud of her two puppies, as she referred to them, and enjoyed showing them off in her sexy, two-piece bathing suit. Even though she knew her face looked much older now than when she and Dink went to school together, she still considered herself an attractive woman and hadn't gained but about five pounds since then.

Neither of the girls had finished high school. Wanda Faye married at fourteen and Nadine at sixteen. Wanda Faye, however, knew Dink had seen her picture in the *Turpricone News* about three weeks ago, as did everyone in town. She had been awarded her GED, as well as her high school diploma, and she was so proud. She'd always been smart in school, but her daddy, a longtime pulp wood man, didn't put much stock in education, period, and certainly not for girls, so this was a big accomplishment for her.

The twins were now yelling at their mama, "We're hungry! We're hungry!"

Soon, the rest of the kids chimed in. Wanda Faye told her eldest son, Little Chet, to take the children up to the picnic table, get the grocery bag from the car and fix all of them a peanut butter and jelly sandwich.

"They's some of them Oreo cookies in there, too," Wanda Faye said to him. "Plus, a whole big cooler full of sweet iced tea," she added.

Off the children ran. When they were about halfway up the hill, Dink called out.

"Boy! Here!" he shouted, and Little Chet ran back to him. "Take this ten dollar bill and go up to that concession stand and buy you and all them children a cold drink of your choice," he said.

"Thank you, Mr. Dink," Little Chet said, smiling as if he'd just been given a hundred-dollar bill.

Wanda Faye smiled, too, and then turned her float toward Dink so she could see his face.

"Sho' was nice of you, Dink," she said. "Thank you."

Dink waved his hand toward her, indicating she should think nothing of it. Then, he pointed to the plastic baggie she had in her lap.

"Can I bum a cigarette from you?" he asked. "I don't smoke much, but once in a while I like to smoke one when I'm relaxing."

Wanda Faye pulled a cigarette out, lit it for him, and then handed it to him.

"Smoke all you want, baby. We got plenty," she said. "Tell us, you old handsome thing, how you been? We ain't seen you in a coon's age."

"Well, you know Byronelle left me and ran off with that Randy Preston... you know, he was raised out there near Winfield," Dink said, as he drew in a puff of smoke. "I wondered why he started bringing his stock car to me to work on, and hanging out so much down there at the Smokin' Pig where Byronelle was waitin' tables. Hell, next news I got, she wrote me a letter and left it on the nightstand. Told me she wanted more outta life. I tell you, it threw me for a loop. I stayed drunk for about a week. When I sobered up, I said to myself, just get over it and be thankful they ain't no youngun's. See, that was one of our troubles. I ain't able, you know, because of them mumps goin' down on me when I was about five years old, and Byronelle, well, she wanted a baby."

Wanda Faye and Nadine were both sipping on their drinks, as they intently listened to Dink's story. Nadine took a long drag off her cigarette, and looked him straight in the eyes.

"Well, Dink, honey," she said. "Mama always says God has a reason for everything. Byronelle knew all about you when she married you. Knowing you, I know they weren't no secrets. I'll tell you, most of these women today ain't got the Holy Ghost in their hearts. All they want is what a man can give 'em. No thought for anyone but themself."

Dink nodded in agreement.

"I sho' ain't done right in a lot of ways, but I've tried to stick with Louie," Nadine went on. "Believe me, it ain't been easy with him being partially disabled, and us living off my salary, and what little he gets from Workman's Comp."

"I'm sure it's been really tough on you, Nadine," Dink said.

"I wish that damned Carl Alvin Campbell would get his cousin to work on my case," Nadine continued rambling. "I've talked and talked to him, but so far, I ain't seen a thing. My teeth's giving me trouble and all the children need to go to the dentist in the worst way. I wish he'd get his cousin, Hugh Jr. on the go."

"Carl Alvin or C.A., as he likes to be called," Dink began, exaggerating the initials. "Well, he ain't gonna get in no hurry, honey, as long as old man Hamp's bailing him out of his messes 'cause he's buying too many clothes and shoes, and buying too much liquor and, from what I hear, salve... you know, cocaine. He ain't gonna be in no hurry."

"You don't have to tell me," Nadine piped up, shaking her head.

"He's always runnin' 'round playing southern gentleman," Dink said. "I'm here to tell you, he ain't in that office up in Turpricone but about a day and a half a week. He's either gallivantin' over in Tallahassee or down in Miamuh, or taking some trip to Europe or the islands, or down to Mexico. Only man I ever seen who spends more on his fingernails and toenails, gettin' his hair dyed and havin' facials than most women I know. All the women's crazy about him, though, but he ain't never with one on a steady basis. You know... well, I ain't gonna say, but they's rumors."

"Now, hold on a minute, Dink!" Wanda Faye said, shaking her lit cigarette between her fingers at him. "You're a good friend and an old one, but I ain't gonna listen to that kinda talk. Carl Alvin's a good man and he helped me get out of that mess up in Georgia with Chester."

Dink seemed taken aback at Wanda Faye's

tone and it showed on his face.

"Didn't mean to rile you so, Wanda Faye," he said. "Just statin' what I'd heard is all. Carl Alvin ain't never been nothin' but nice to me. I gotta say he's got a hell of an outgoin' personality. Life of the party, you know. He just ain't, well, you know, always been real manly, but I never seen him queer off with nobody. If that's his thing, though, and if that's what he wants, as long as he don't try that mess with me, more power, I say."

Hearing a commotion at the top of the hill, the trio swung around to look. Coming down the hill were Darlene and Charlene, both holding big, green bottles of Mountain Dew and heading back to the swimming hole. Following them was Trixie, the little Chihuahua that was the favored pet of Wanda Faye's children. Trixie jumped right in the water with them, but immediately began to shiver. She spotted Wanda Faye and paddled over to her with her big, brown saucer eyes trained on her float.

"Trixie, sweet baby," Wanda Faye said, reaching over to coddle the little mutt. "Yes, darling, you're mama's baby, ain't you?"

Dink started laughing and both girls joined in.

"Go on, honey," Wanda Faye said, and she turned the dog toward the shore. "Go on and get out of the water, baby," she added, and off Trixie paddled.

"Look at that little thing," Dink said, grinning as he watched her paddle toward the shore. "She ain't afraid of nothin'. Ma always said if them little dogs weighed ninety pounds, the world would be in a whole lotta danger."

"She's a good, little watch dog," Wanda Faye said. "She lets us know if anything comes 'round. With all that trash hangin' 'round at them apartments where I live, all kinds of trash... black, white and Mexicans. I ain't gonna single out the blacks, 'cause some of them others is just as damned sorry."

Dink raised his eyebrows at her.

"Excuse me, Dink, for cussing," she said. "I'm trying to do better on that. That reminds me, Nadine, we can't soak much longer. We gotta get ready to leave. We got that revival to go to tonight. We promised Mama, and she'll be lookin' for us. I already talked to Destini. You remember our best friend, Destini Wilson, don't you Dink?" she asked, turning back toward him. "I don't know what we'd do without her. She's always so good to help us out with the children."

"Yes," Dink said. "How in the world could I forget Destini? Lord, when y'all was growin' up and would bring her to church with you, those out-of-town folks gawked at y'all with their eyes as wide as big ol' turkey platters. Two little white girls and Destini dark as Egypt, walkin' in with y'all. That Destini sure is a hoot, though. I've always liked her."

"She's a treasure," Wanda Faye said. "She lives out at her mama's place at Buckeye Bay. She's got a youngun herself, a little girl named Easter Bunnye, almost five years old. We're gonna take a bunch of frozen pizzas and some movies out there later, and they'll all have a good time."

Dink suddenly turned and paddled over to the diving dock. After he hoisted himself up, he swung around, held his arms out and performed a perfect swan dive into the water. Wanda Faye laughed, thinking he was acting like a young teenager who was trying to impress his girlfriend. Seconds later, he was back to where the girls were floating.

"Ma, God rest her soul, always said you girls was hard workers and raised right by your mama, Miss Jewell," Dink said out of the blue. "If ever they was a sanctified, righteous woman, I believe it's her."

"Well, thank you, Dink," Nadine said. "Yeah, Mama's righteous, sanctified, and can out-pray the blessed Apostle Paul, but Lord knows that strap of hers had some powerful hell fire in it for me and Wanda Faye when we was growin' up. Not that we didn't deserve it. We ran poor ol' Mama a merry race. Not bad stuff, just slippin' off with the boys, who we shoulda left alone, smokin' cigarettes, drinkin' beer, comin' home late, but Mama did her best with us. Like that song by Merle Haggard that Daddy liked so good, Mama tried."

"Well, at least y'all didn't turn twenty-one in the slammer doin' life without parole, like the song says," Dink piped up.

Nadine sighed. "No, we didn't, Dink. We didn't go to prison, but we both had three or four youngun's by the time we turned twenty-one. Lord, I wish I'd listened to them teachers up there at the elementary school when they tried to tell me about goin' to school."

Dink swam over closer to Wanda Faye and asked for another cigarette. Wanda Faye figured he just wanted to check her out some more, which made her smile. She lit up another cigarette and handed it to him.

"Here you go, hon," she said. "By the way, I was so sorry to hear about your mama passin' earlier this year."

"Yeah, that ol' cancer finally done her in," Dink said, as his eyes teared up. "Now, she's up in heaven with my daddy, probably drivin' him nuts."

"I don't doubt it," Wanda Faye said. "Them two was quite a team, always teasin' each other."

Wanda Faye and Dink had a small fling just a few months before she and Chester got married. In fact, Dink had lost his virginity to her, and she lost hers to him. It happened not far down the road from the House of Prayer, the church they attended in Seraph Springs.

She recalled when both their mothers had gone to a revival meeting in the early fall that year and brought all the kids with them. It started about five in the afternoon on a Saturday, and included supper and then a sing-along. At about six or six-thirty, Dink got up from the pew where he was sitting and went outside. On his way out, he looked over in Wanda Faye's direction and winked at her. She took the hint and followed him seconds later.

The two of them walked down Eldridge Street and cut up a little creek that ran through the north part of town. There, in a clearing surrounded by palmettos and gall berries, they discovered the pleasures of the flesh, as the preacher called it. In fact, before they were through, they had discovered that pleasure about four times. At one point, Wanda Faye even told him she loved him and he said it back to her.

She remembered being worried about him not using protection that day, until he told her about the mumps problem he had. After they cleaned up and lay there for a bit, they enjoyed the pleasures of the flesh one last time before returning to the church where, coincidentally or not, the pastor was preaching about fornication.

For the remainder of that church service, Wanda Faye knew in her heart that Dink was thinking about nothing else except the wonderful time the two of them just had together, exactly like she was doing. Would it be the last time? She didn't know then, and she didn't know now.

Not long after their naughty little tryst down by the creek, Wanda Faye traveled up to Ludowici, Georgia to supposedly go to high school there and help her aunt, Alma Ruth, in her café. It was there she met Chester Easley, a mechanic at her uncle's garage next door to the café.

Chester was twenty-four, had been in the military, had driven an 18-wheeler across the country, had his own single-wide trailer just outside Ludowici, and he played electric bass in the church ensemble at the Ludowici House of Prayer. Wanda Faye and Alma Ruth never missed a service.

It wasn't long before Wanda Faye figured out Chester was interested in her. There was one small problem, though. Wanda Faye just found out she was pregnant.

Chapter 2

The tale Dink had told Wanda Faye about not being able to father a child, which even his mama believed, was either an outright lie or the doctor had gotten something horribly wrong. Wanda Faye knew she had to do something... and fast.

Dink wasn't old enough to marry her, and neither her mother nor Aunt Alma Ruth would ever consider allowing her to have an abortion. When she looked at Chester, the tall, gangly, bass-player, she surmised he wasn't too bright, but at least he seemed somewhat steady. She figured since leaving the church and enjoying the pleasures of the flesh had worked once, she could do it again.

Ludowici wasn't much more advanced than Seraph Springs and so, on an early fall night, not ten weeks after Chester had shown her that first sign of interest, she went to church, but not for sanctification. She went for what she hoped would be her salvation.

Alma Ruth, along with the preacher's wife, Sister Marie, and their daughter, the obese, high-haired, piano-playing Doris Ann, were in the middle of performing "Heaven's Jubilee" when Wanda Faye walked into the church Sunday evening. She watched as Doris Ann made google-eyes at Chester and realized time was of the essence, especially when he smiled back at the chubby Doris Ann.

Not long after the preaching started, Wanda Faye got up from her seat to go to the ladies room. On her way past where Chester was sitting on the aisle-side of the second pew from the back, she made sure he was watching her as she lightly touched her breast, and then she coyly smiled at him. She hurried outside to the bathroom, which was a small cinder block structure just beyond the church a few yards to the left.

As she sat down to take care of business, she prayed, "Dear, God, let him be outside this door when I go out."

When she emerged minutes later, she spotted Chester ambling around by the water fountain just a few feet away from the bathroom door.

"Sho' did play good tonight, Chester," she said. "I always love hearing you play the bass guitar."

"Well, thank you, Wanda Faye," he said, blushing. "I'ze thankin' maybe you'd like to take a little walk before we go back inside. I know I'd like to wind down just a second. After playing for a while, a little walk seems to do the trick for me."

As he spoke, Wanda Faye studied him from head to toe. He had mousy brown hair, sky-blue eyes, a slack jaw, and not much of a chin. He was actually cadaver-like, she thought, and he had the biggest hands and feet she'd ever seen on a man. He had good teeth, although, one of his front teeth was lopped over top of the other tooth. From what she knew of him, he didn't smoke, though, which she figured might be an issue down the road.

"I'll deal with that later," she thought.

For a mechanic, she noticed he kept his hands and nails unusually clean. Uncle Earl and the boys at the garage sometimes made fun of him, she'd heard from her aunt, but not too much. They'd say, "Chet is sho' funny about his hands, but maybe that's 'cause he plays the bass guitar."

Wanda Faye knew both his parents were dead. His mama died in childbirth with him, and his daddy was killed in a car wreck coming from Waycross, where he worked at the rail yard.

"Yes, Chet, I'll walk with you up the road a piece, if walkin's all you got on your mind," Wanda Faye told him.

At that, she giggled a little to let him know she would go further. He was a little slow on the uptake, however, because it took him a good fifteen minutes to get his hands out of his pockets and reach out to hold her hand. It took him another ten minutes before he shyly asked if he could kiss her. When she agreed, and he did kiss her, she could feel his hardness press against her. She was surprised that for a full grown man, his "business" was not nearly what Dink's had been.

They went out into the woods, across a little pond, and there she let him take her. He said he was a little surprised she wasn't a virgin, but she told him it had happened riding the old horse her daddy had. He seemed satisfied.

After their sexual escapade, the two of them walked down to a small creek where they cleaned up. As they were putting on their clothes, Chester turned to her.

"I think we should marry," he said. "I love you, and I know I'm the first one. I want to be the only one. Would you marry me?"

Wanda Faye was floored that he would propose so quickly. She hemmed and hawed for a bit to make things look authentic, but minutes later she agreed. Even though they had just met and a marriage proposal so quickly was insane, to say the least, she knew she had to do it, or else risk the shame of being an unwed mother at the ripe young age of fourteen.

What she didn't know, unfortunately, was that saying "Yes" to Chester would turn out to be the biggest mistake of her life.

Three weeks later, she put on a good show and tearfully told him she thought she was pregnant. The two were married the Saturday after Thanksgiving at the House of Prayer in Ludowici. Wanda Faye's parents agreed to sign for her to marry, because Chester was a church-going boy and could play the bass guitar like a member of Gabriel's angel band.

The newly-knotted couple took a short honeymoon trip to Jekyll Island. They chose a Comfort Inn not far from the beach, because Wanda Faye said she had never been to the beach before. After they arrived, they ate fried shrimp in the motel restaurant. Before she could swallow the last sip of tea, Chester grabbed her by the hand and the two of them ran to their room to further consummate the marriage.

That night, all she felt was relief when the act was over, but she was experienced enough that she knew to say at the end, "That was so good, baby. You are such a man." She'd read that line once in an article inside a borrowed *True Story* magazine and it seemed to work like a charm on Chester.

When the baby arrived in early June, most of his facial features – a high forehead, perky nose and prominent chin – looked more like her than Dink, and she was glad of that. He did have Dink's sandy hair, though. The most glaring feature was his eyes. They were Dink's through and through; a deep blue, almost the color of the sky on an overcast day. He also had Dink's long eyelashes that seemed such a waste on a boy, she thought. The fact that he weighed only a little over five pounds helped Wanda Faye with her deception. She swore to everyone that he came two months early and everybody believed her.

Chester turned out to be a proud daddy and took his Little Chet with him to the store, to church and, every once in a while, he'd even let the boy join his parents on the rare occasions when they went out to eat at a restaurant.

Not long after the marriage, Wanda Faye began to see another side of Chester Easley. It was a jealous and self absorbed side. He started making her wear skirts and dresses that came down to the floor, long sleeved blouses and shirts, just like the old women at the Ludowici House of Prayer, and she couldn't wear makeup. He even went so far as to rake their sand-filled yard before going off to work, so he could check for strange footprints on the ground when he got back home. Wanda Faye stayed at home most of the time, at least until noon, because Chester would come home to eat lunch every day just to check up on her.

Aunt Alma Ruth's house was her only refuge. She was allowed to go there twice a week for the women's evening Bible study class. Once there, she would slip letters to her friend, Marcy Simmons, a peroxide blonde who worked in the restaurant for her aunt. Every once in a while they'd have some alone time together to chat. She recalled the first time Marcy told her how mean Chester could be.

"They say that's the reason his mama died in childbirth," Marcy said. "It was because of all them beatings his ol' daddy gave her while she was carrying him. He was raised by his grandma, Addie Easley, who was, without a doubt, one of the meanest old cusses ever lived in Ludowici. She took pleasure in poisoning dogs for no reason and torturing little animals, even kittens."

Marcy told her Addie would go over to the House of Prayer and shout down the aisles for no good reason. Not only did she treat small animals like dirt, but kids, too, including all the children she watched for the working mothers around Ludowici.

"They say when she caught Chester playing with himself – the way boys will do when they reach a certain age – she soaked his hands in hot lye water till his nails began to flake off," Marcy said. "That's the reason he's so obsessed with his hands."

Wanda Faye had been clearly taken aback by those revelations and it showed on her face.

"Avanelle Simmons, a doctor's wife up in Brunswick, who Addie used to care for, broke down at the last class reunion we had here," Marcy continued. "She told me the old woman made her eat her own poop and wash out her own underwear before she ever started school. She said Addie swore if she told her mama or Sheriff Simmons, she'd chop her in little pieces."

"Oh, my God!" Wanda Faye gasped.

"Avanelle would never go in the Red Rabbit Grocery Store, the dime store or anywhere if she saw Addie's Chevy parked outside."

"I don't blame her," Wanda Faye said.

"When Addie came to our eighth grade graduation and Avanelle saw her in the audience, she fainted. Yep, fainted and fell off the risers. I tell you, you be careful, girl. That bunch has a loose screw, and I don't mean just a couple... a whole hardware store full."

Years passed. In fact, seven years flew by like a bad nightmare. During that time, Wanda Faye endured beatings, verbal abuse, and the birth of three more children.

Throughout those years, Chester was good to the children and he was a good provider. He never beat her when the children were around. It was always the lunchtime breaks from the garage she dreaded.

It was then, when the wire coat hangers would rattle inside the closet she tried to hide in, that she would break out in hives. He would beat her with his belt until she was welted and screaming. Then, he'd throw her onto the bed and forcefully have sex with her, all the while crying and saying, "I love you, honey. You know I love you. I didn't mean to hurt you. I love you."

For Wanda Faye, there was no ecstasy in the sex. There wasn't even the least bit of pleasure, only dread. As she endured it, she prayed that one day she'd be able to say to some man, somewhere, in return to his lovemaking, "I love you," the same way she had said it to Dink so many years ago.

Chapter 3

After a fun day at Blue Hole Spring with the kids, Wanda Faye and Nadine arrived at Destini's house in Buckeye Bay. The house looked rather like a long, crazy maze. There were four single-wide trailers of various sizes and shapes, which had been interconnected by a series of shelters and walkways. It allowed all her nieces and nephews, and her one precocious five-year-old, Easter Bunnye, who was born on Easter Sunday five years ago, to run and play from one house to the other.

Destini's nephew, a carpenter of sorts, had built a screened porch that ran the length of all four trailers. In front of the screens were old trellises that were built long ago, and they were thickly covered with morning glory vines and Confederate jasmine. To observe it from the street, the unusual trailer arrangement looked like a colorful blue and white shade loggia during the late spring and summer, as honey bees and hummingbirds darted in and out of the scented blossoms.

Flanking each side of the trailer arrangement were two huge mimosa trees drenched with pink, powder puff blossoms. Here, too, the butterflies, bees and hummingbirds performed beautiful aerial ballets. The yard itself was bare of grass. None could grow there, as so many children played back and forth in it all the time.

At the edge of the clearing in the backyard was an antique pitcher pump that had been left intact. It pumped some of the coolest, most refreshing water in the south end of Campbell County. When Wanda Faye and Nadine were kids, their mama would often come out to fill plastic gallon jugs full of water to use for iced tea. Destini's grandmother, Mama Tee, swore the water from that well made the best iced tea in the world, which many in Seraph Springs would testify as being the truth.

In the first trailer, sitting in an old lounger in a back room, was Mama Tee. Nobody knew exactly how old she was, since she had no recorded birth certificate.

Before she collected social security in the mid seventies, Judge John Wesson had taken a deposition and determined she had been born around 1910. She told him she was a good, big girl when Jim Campbell, for whom her mother worked and on whose farm she had been born, marched off to the "big war across the pond." Destini, her brothers and sisters, and the older nieces and nephews took care of Mama Tee, fixing her meals and attending to her needs.

Mama Tee's eyesight had been gone for many years because of her losing battle with "sugar in the blood", as she called it. She always wore dark sunglasses, but her mind was as clear as a bell. Even without the use of her eyes, she could identify each of her children, grandchildren, great grandchildren, nieces and nephews, and great nieces and nephews just by hearing their voices or inhaling their distinct scents.

In her younger days, she had been an ample woman, weighing over two-hundred pounds. She was able, according to Wanda Faye and Nadine's daddy, to hold her own with anyone, man or woman.

A church going woman all her life, Mama Tee won the respect of all in her community many years ago in the way she dealt with her husband, Junior, and his infidelity.

One hot, summer afternoon, without saying a word to anyone, she walked the six miles into the downtown area of Seraph Springs and went inside the bar where Junior and his woman were "juking it up".

Mama Tee eased up to the woman and sliced her so thoroughly with a straight razor that the woman never completely recovered. From that point on, Mama Tee was given a wide berth by all in the small river community. She told Mr. Lucius Lee once that she never tried to be a mean, bad woman, but that she always meant to hold on to what was hers.

Wanda Faye and Nadine had just walked into Mama Tee's kitchen and set down ten frozen pizzas on the counter next to the refrigerator. They had also brought with them several packets of strawberry flavored Kool Aid, and a five pound bag of Dixie Dandy sugar, as well as four frozen, plastic gallon jugs of ice, so that Destini and the kids could break it up. Then, all the children could have ice cold Kool Aid with their pizzas.

The kitchen was filled with the aroma of Destini's famous buttermilk biscuits which, along with her homemade jellies, jams and cane syrup, would serve as dessert for the kids. She had also made two huge pans of Rice Krispy treats.

The children were already outside playing hide-and-go-seek, and through the screened windows could be heard the shouts of, "Ready or not, here I come!" accompanied by squeals and giddy laughter.

Destini came into the kitchen and motioned toward Mama Tee's room.

"See how she lookin' around?" Destini asked Wanda Faye and Nadine. "She know y'all be here. Go on in and speak to her."

Wanda Faye went in first, followed by Nadine. Mama Tee immediately sat up straight and her head began moving from side to side. In a split second, a knowing smile came across her face. She reached beside her chair for the empty Maxwell House coffee can and spat a huge stream of tobacco juice into it. Mama Tee loved her Railroad Mills snuff and had dipped it most of her life.

Lifting her head higher, she said, "Wanda Faye, Nadine, come on over here and hug Mama Tee's neck. I declare it sho' is good to see bof you girls. Sweet babies y'all was when Miss Jewell would bring y'all out here as small chirrun for me to watch over, and still sweet babies now. Is that y'all's babies I hear playin' and laughin' outside?"

Both girls hugged the old lady and, in turn, answered, "Yes, ma'am. That's our babies."

"You look after them Mama Tee, and let us know if they sass Destini or get ugly," Wanda Fay told her.

With that, the old lady began to laugh.

"I heah yah," she said. "Where you gals off to? Mighty perfumed up. Y'all going to church or the club? I hope it's the church, 'cause them clubs can sho' cause troubles."

"Yes'm, we're goin' to the revival down at Mama's church," Nadine said. "We promised her we would go."

"Well, praise de Lawd," Mama Tee said, almost shouting. "I've worried over you chirrun, 'specially you, Wanda Faye. Is you still watchin' my gal on the television? You know who I'm talking 'bout. My baby. Not mine by blood, but my TV adopted baby."

"You talkin' about Margot Smith?" Wanda Faye asked, as she lovingly held Mama Tee's hands.

"Who else you think I'm talkin' 'bout?" Mama Tee teased her. "She's an angel sent from the Lawd, that chile. Sho' as heaven's happy, she is one sweet lady. I loves her. I cain't see her, but I listen, and you can tell a lot about a person's heart by jest listenin'."

"You sho' can," Nadine piped up.

"Just like you, Wanda Faye," Mama Tee continued. "Nobody had to tell me you was broken mighty low when you came home last year from up there in Georgia, but I knew. I could hear it. I cain't see, but I can tell. Let me feel them wrists, girl. Uh-humm, more meat on dem bones now. That's a good sign, baby. Jesus is satisfied with you. Are you still watchin' my baby on TV, Wanda Faye?" the old woman asked again to make sure Wanda Faye was keeping the faith.

As Wanda Faye nodded, Mama Tee felt her face and knew she was crying, as it was wet with tears.

"Yes'm, I'm still watching her ever' day," Wanda Faye said. "When I was up in Georgia, Miss Margot was the only one, other than the Savior himself that kept me from goin' crazy.

There was days I couldn't hardly get a hold of myself, and I would pray and ask Jesus to help me make it just a little further. Then, Miss Margot would come on the television. Just listenin' to her helped me so much. I ain't a good writer, Mama Tee, but if I was, I'd write and tell her how much she's meant to me."

"You ain't gotta write, baby," Mama Tee told her. "Jest pray for her. We all needs prayer, even my baby, Margot. Sometimes, them you thinks has got it all carries a mighty heavy cross on the inside. Pray for her, baby. You'll get a blessin' and so will she."

"Yes'm, I will Mama Tee. I'll pray for you, too. Will you pray for me?"

"Baby, I already is prayed for you and my Nadine, and my sweet Destini and all my babies. Prayed for my TV baby, too, yes, ma'am. Prayed for all y'all several times today, jest like I do ever' day." She pointed her bony finger toward heaven and said, "Me and the old boss man, we on a first name basis. Yes, ma'am, we knows each other real well. Y'all go on, now, and don't forget to pray for your mama's... both of us. Ehhh, Lawd Jesus."

With that, the old lady chuckled again and began humming a tune. Every once in a while, she'd softly sing, "A charge to keep I have."

The girls said their goodbye's and eased out the door and into the yard moments later. They waved to Destini, and then Nadine called over to

Little Chet, Victor, Darlene and Charlene, and told them in front of Destini that she could tear them up till their behinds roked like okra if they didn't behave. To prove it, she handed Destini a couple of cured gall berry switches.

"No, no, ladies," Destini said. "This ain't no bring your own switch party. No, ma'am. I got my own right up there on that porch."

Destini pointed to an old ceramic crock sitting next to the front door that held a number of switches of various sizes and shapes, and in various stages of curing.

"All right," Nadine said. "I see you got it under control."

With that, the girls hopped into the old long-bed Ford camper pickup. Wanda Faye fired it up and off they went to church. On the way, they didn't talk much. It was as if they were both contemplating what Mama Tee had told them. Nadine lit up her second cigarette just as they got to the north gate of the state park.

She turned to Wanda Faye and said, "I feel like I been to church already. Being with Mama Tee always makes me feel that way."

Wanda Faye nodded, took a drag from her own cigarette, blew smoke through her nose, and said, "We ought to be liftin' her up, and instead, she lifts us up ever' time. I tell you, Nadine, when that old woman goes to glory, it's gonna be hard on me. I don't love... *really* love too many people outside my blood family, but I sho' do love Mama Tee. With my whole heart, I love her."

Nadine grabbed a bottle of Tabu cologne spray from her purse and then turned to her sister.

"We'd better souse down pretty good, so Mama won't smell so much of this cigarette smoke on us. You know how she gives us down the river about smoking," Nadine said.

"And you think sprayin' yourself down is goin' to make Mama think you ain't been smoking?" Wanda Faye replied with a snort and a chuckle. "Devil, Nadine! Mama may be old, but she ain't crazy!"

Chapter 4

After Wanda Faye parked the pickup, both she and Nadine emerged from the cab dressed in pencil skirts that fell way below the knee. Nadine's skirt was black and Wanda Faye's was navy blue. They both wore long-sleeved blouses with high necks and on their legs were dark stockings. The only showy piece of attire was their shoes. They were black patent leather, stiletto heels with ankle straps. Around each girl's left ankle was a sterling silver anklet with a heart engraved with their respective names. Nadine had purchased them at a jewelry store, on sale, of course, over in Pittstown a couple years back and had them engraved at the store.

Their hair always required a lot of ministration before church, in order to pass their mother's standards. They teased it and put on hair pieces, so that their hair stood high in a big, teased bun with tendrils streaming down their backs. This type hairdo could make those who were not righteous followers of the Master at least appear to be righteous.

Raised in the strict admonition of the Pentecostal church, the girls were groomed as was befitting the respect they held for their beloved mama, who was a pillar of the church. Neither of them wore any makeup, except a slight brushing of mascara.

As they entered the church, Brother Otis Linton and his wife, Sister Velma, met them at the door and hugged them tightly.

"Oh, my Lord, Velma, would you lookie here?" Otis exclaimed, as he stepped back and eyed Nadine and Wanda Faye. "Seems just yesterday y'all was hidin' and huntin' Easter eggs for Jerri Faye, bless her little heart. She keeps pictures of you two girls on her nightstand and kisses them goodnight every single night."

"She sho' does," Velma said. "She's always loved you girls. We all have. Y'all go up and speak to her. She'll be so happy to see both of y'all."

Jerri Faye Linton was sitting behind the girls' mother, Miss Jewell, whose piled-high, gray and white, voluminous bun jutted above Jerri Faye's little round head with her mousy brown pixie cut she'd sported forever. When she turned towards the girls, a big, knowing smile crossed her face and she poked Miss Jewell in the back.

"Wannie and Nay Nay! Wannie and Nay Nay!" she squealed, which prompted Miss Jewell to turn around and shush her.

“Jerri Faye, calm down, baby,” Miss Jewell said. “They’re coming, precious. They’re coming.”

Jerri Faye was well past the age of twenty-five and older than both the girls. When they got closer, she grabbed them both and threw her arms around their shoulders in a display of unconditional love, characteristic of many children with Down’s syndrome.

After years of praying and raising countless numbers of foster children, including nieces and nephews, Sister Velma discovered she was pregnant at the age of forty-one. According to Miss Jewell, Velma and Otis knew Jerri Faye would be one of God’s special angels, and that her time on earth wouldn’t be long.

The doctors told the Lintons her heart was so damaged that she likely wouldn’t make it past age eighteen, but here she was at twenty-five, still happy, and still very much loved by her parents and the members of the little church, as well as her schoolmates and teachers.

Each day for Jerri Faye was a new adventure, and life, each moment of it, held limitless possibilities. No service at Seraph Springs House of Prayer was complete without her singing “Jesus Loves Me”. When she’d get to the chorus, she would signal for everyone to join in.

Both girls hugged and kissed Jerri Faye and told her how beautiful she looked. Her dress was a pale pink with a huge bow in the back. It was the same style she had worn since she was a little girl. Most all of her dresses were either pink or red, as they were her two favorite colors.

"Sit wif me, sit wif me," Jerri Faye squealed, and she patted the bench on each side of her for them to sit down.

Both Wanda Faye and Nadine knew they'd only be sitting there temporarily because Sister Velma would be around shortly to take over. She'd have to sit with Jerri Faye to keep her calm when the preaching reached a fever pitch, which it always did around halfway through the sermon. Sister Velma knew, as only a mother would, when to take Jerri Faye outside and let her have a break from the service, when to take her to the ladies room, and how to touch her arm and caress it to reassure her. This relationship between mother and daughter was truly one of Christian love in action.

After chatting with Jerri Faye for a few minutes, Wanda Faye spotted Otis and Velma coming towards them.

"Oh, look, Jerri Faye, it's not even Mother's Day, but we're gonna play Mother's Day, precious. You sit with your mother and we're going to sit with ours, because we love our mamas, don't we, honey?"

"Yeth, Yeth, we do love our mamas, Wannie. Don't we love them, Nay, Nay? We're gonna be good girls and sit with our mamas, cauth we're playing Movver's Day."

Sister Velma overheard the exchange between the girls and she winked at Wanda Faye, mouthing a silent, "thank you" at the same time. Wanda Faye nodded her head and reciprocated with a silent, "I love you." Sister Velma clutched her heart and then dabbed her eyes with her lace-trimmed handkerchief.

As Velma took over, Nadine and Wanda Faye moved up to where their mama was sitting and they both embraced her. Miss Jewell began sniffling at the sight of them, which she always did each time they came to a special church service. The girls gave each other a knowing look and braced themselves for her waterworks.

Turning to Sister Velma, Miss Jewell said, "These two mean more to me than all the diamonds and gold in the world. Oh, thank you, Jesus, thank you, Jesus," she added under her breath, although, it was loud enough so the others around her could hear.

Velma smiled at her. Meanwhile, Wanda Faye rolled her eyes at Nadine, who slyly winked back at her, as the two of them watched their mother play church.

Wanda Faye knew, however, that her mama took the sermons seriously while she was in the house of the Lord, and she could quote scripture as well as any preacher or evangelist. For thirty years, she taught the women's Sunday school class, was the head of the Women's Missionary Circle, and served as the coach for the Bible Drill team.

For twenty-five years straight, her Bible Drill team from little Seraph Springs House of Prayer earned the championship each year for all of Florida and Georgia. The preacher said it was a miracle, but Wanda Faye was certain he knew about the threats and whippings her mama would dole out to her little soldiers, as well as all the visits she made to their homes. Mama had a way of convincing the parents she was the reincarnation of Angel Gabriel and Mary Magdalene, all rolled into one.

She prayed with the parents, all the while telling them she was doing the Lord's work, and that only discipline and a solid three to four months of dedicating each Friday and Saturday to slumber parties and lock-ins at the church fellowship hall with her to practice Bible verses would bring victory in Jesus.

Other than short breaks to eat, she made her little soldiers watch short documentaries made by the National Pentecostal Office with titles such as, "Hell: Do you Want to Go There?" or "This is Hell", which was one of the scariest videos. It came complete with flames consuming flesh and people burning to death. Oftentimes, this one was shown until about two weeks before the annual drill, in order to keep everyone's mind on the heat of the battle.

Miss Jewell was a general in the army of the Lord, Wanda Faye thought. She was a stalwart, disciplined general, who expected and received absolute obedience. Nothing other than that was tolerated. She considered herself as holy and righteous a woman as there could be in the church, and she very seldom admitted backsliding.

She loved all the scriptures, especially the one about the first being last and the last being first when it came to the finances of some around her, whom she considered weren't doing right by the Lord and His church. When it came to her Bible Drill team, however, she didn't apply that particular scripture.

Miss Jewell lived, ate, and breathed the church day and night, night and day. On occasion, when the real world entered her Pentecostal utopia, she reacted with venom and downright meanness. She was intolerant of anyone who didn't think like her, believe like her, or dress like her. Frequently, in the privacy of their homes, she referred to the matrons – the wives and daughters of prominent farmers and timber businessmen in Campbell County – as the "painted harlots of Babylon".

The first time she saw Wanda Faye and Nadine painted and powdered up in front of the movie theater in Pittstown, she screamed at them and prayed all the way home.

Once they got home, she'd fall on the floor and twist up like a shot snake, all the while shouting, "Help me bear it, Jesus! Help me bear it! You know I've done my duty as a mother. Oh, Lord, soften the heart of the disobedient child."

Once the scripture quoting was over, the gall berry switch came out, and she swung it with venom and vengeance, letting it strike where it may. When it did strike with all the force of her nearly two-hundred-and-fifty pounds behind it, it didn't just hurt, it was agony.

Sister Mary Lee Walters had just sat down at the piano off to the side of the pulpit and the congregation quieted down. Mary Lee was a tall, emaciated looking woman with sharp features, who had worn the same style of eyeglasses since Wanda Faye could remember. They had cat eyes on the frame with blue inset jewels for the cat's eyeballs. She was an expert seamstress and often made floor length, polyester dresses for herself with long voile sleeves to wear for special services.

Her spiritual hero for many years, she said, was the late Kathryn Kuhlman. Several years back, she publicly sobbed when the church gave her a complete set of DVD's of all of Kathryn Kuhlman's shows and revivals. It was a gift for thirty years of service as the church pianist.

Often when Brother Linton was going to pray for healing, Sister Mary Lee would play the piano in the background and softly sing Kathryn's famous, "I Believe in Miracles".

Tonight, Mary Lee was wearing a subdued, lilac, floor length gown with a high neck and full sleeves that ballooned over her arms and came together in a long cuff at her wrists. As she played the piano, the sleeves moved with grace and beauty, Wanda Faye thought, and she said so to her mother.

Mama made a face and said, "She's just trying to draw attention to herself. She needs to read and study the scripture about the lowly publican. Yes, Jesus."

Wanda Faye figured the real reason her mama held such disdain for Mary Lee was because she was jealous of her thin physique. She'd never admit it, of course, but she was definitely jealous. Many times, she commented how Mary Lee, at every church supper, ate like it was her last meal, often consuming two plates of desserts.

One time, as she was eating the last bites of a big slice of chocolate cake, she cast her eyes at Miss Jewell and said, "I guess I'm just blessed with an overactive metabolism. I can eat whatever I want, and I have never been a stout woman a day in my life."

Another time, Miss Jewell's face turned bright red with embarrassment and anger when

Mary Lee commented on her dress.

"Oh, Miss Jewell, that's a beautiful black dress you're wearing, honey. I always say black is so elegant and so slimming, too," she said.

Every once in a while, though, Miss Jewell would admit that Mary Lee could really make a piano talk, like tonight, for instance, as she played one of her favorites, "I'll Have a New Body." Miss Jewell sang the words, as the notes lilted from the ivory keys.

"On that resurrection morning when the redeemed in Christ shall rise,

I'll have a new body, praise the Lord, I'll have a new life.

Sown in the likeness of his image, ever to live in paradise,

I'll have a new body. Praise the Lord, I'll have a new life."

When Mary Lee came to the chorus, the piano keys took on a life of their own. By this time, there was clapping, stomping of feet, and nodding of heads throughout the congregation. Mary Lee was getting everyone in the spirit with an attitude of praise, and ready to receive the Word of God.

When the song ended, Brother Linton welcomed everyone to the revival. After prayer and announcements, he set about introducing the speaker, Brother Eugene Martin.

"I've known Gene for many years," he said.

"God rest their souls, I had the privilege and honor of preaching the funeral services for his beloved daddy and mama after tragedy struck. They both lost their lives in a car accident traveling from their home in Bonifay up to Elba, Alabama, where they were leading a revival meeting."

Several in the congregation began to weep as they listened to Brother Linton. Wanda Faye was crying, too, as she fondly remembered the Martins from her childhood. They had always conducted special services for the children and gave each child a honey bun when the service was over. They said all the blessed little children were their "Honey Buns".

Wanda Faye hadn't seen Gene in many years and she was surprised at what a fine looking, young man he had become. He had always been a rather plain child.

Gone were the thick, horn-rimmed glasses of his youth, and his freckles and reddish blonde hair, which he had often been teased about, were now somewhat becoming. His hair was fashionably cut and styled, and he was wearing a beautiful, summer poplin suit with a light green shirt and a multi-colored silk tie with shades of the same green. The colors seemed to make his bright, blue eyes come to life. When he smiled in Nadine's direction, Wanda Faye audibly gasped. In place of the braces he'd worn since he was a teenager was the most beautiful set of sparkling white teeth she'd ever seen. He had just enough of a suntan, too, that his smile looked brilliant.

When he began with the first "Beloved", it seemed to Wanda Faye that Nadine wasn't hearing one word of his sermon. She was mesmerized by him. Wanda Faye, on the other hand, hung on to each word he said, which was centered on not looking back to Egypt.

She identified with every bit of what he preached, as she definitely never wanted to look back to her Egypt, which was Chester, the beatings, and that blasted crystal meth house in Ludowici.

As Brother Gene, with an attitude of fire and passion, told about the faith of Moses leading the Hebrew children out of bondage, and how foolish some of them had been, Wanda Faye thought about her own foolishness and naïveté in the days when Chester sent her all over South Georgia buying Sudafed. He made out like it was for missionary packets to send to those serving in the vineyards of the Lord down in Central America and Africa.

Oftentimes, he would hand her two-hundred dollars, saying it came from the church, and he'd send her to Valdosta, Waycross, Brunswick, and down to Pittstown and Barkley to buy Sudafed. Other days, he'd arrange for Aunt Alma Ruth to keep the children and send her to Jacksonville, where she learned the location of every Wal-Mart on the north and west sides of town.

She'd have to sign for the packets of Sudafed and, after being questioned three or four times, she adamantly told the store clerks that she was on a mission for Jesus. Even though many gave her funny looks, most of them never questioned her. In hindsight, she knew that her nearly floor length dresses, no makeup, her necklace with the cross, and the big, white Bible tucked under her arm might have been what kept them from reporting her to the authorities.

Chester bought her the Bible with gold lettering and insisted she take it with her on the trips to the stores, just in case she had the opportunity to share the plan of salvation.

"You never know," he always told her.

She was also fooled when Chester told her he was updating his Grandma Addie's house for them, and that soon, they would move into their newly remodeled home. When he boarded up the windows of the old clapboard house, he told her it was so she couldn't see inside. He wanted it to be a surprise for her, he said. She never had a clue that it was in the kitchen and dining room of the old house that Chester and Sammy Sauls were manufacturing some of the finest crystal meth in the nation.

After Chester was arrested and jailed in Valdosta, Sheriff Carter told her Sammy Sauls, the drummer at the Ludowici House of Prayer, had been involved with manufacturing crystal meth for many years. He said it wasn't until Chester began shooting off his mouth in Waycross and Homerville that he would soon be quitting his job and moving to Honduras, that they were able to catch the two of them red-handed. Chester kept bragging that he was going to start his own church complex, school and village there, and that he and Sammy would be in charge.

What had always puzzled Wanda Faye was why she and the children lived the last three or four days of nearly every week on Ramen Noodles, Showboat Beans and saltines. Sheriff Carter told her they found close to a million dollars buried under the floor of Addie Easley's old smokehouse. Wanda Faye didn't want to believe it at first, but it finally sunk in. It drove home to her even more that Chester never had any real feelings for anyone other than himself.

She stuck with him throughout the trial, but as soon as he began to serve his three-year sentence, she contacted Judge John Wesson, who worked with Preston Holton, an old law school acquaintance of his in Homerville. Holton, with help from Carl Alvin, handled her divorce from Chester. When Wanda Faye agreed that Chester would never have to support any of the children, he gladly signed the papers and told her he never wanted to see her or any of the children again.

Before she left the prison on her last visit with him, she told Chester that Chet Jr. wasn't his child. She also told him that he had never satisfied her sexually, as well as who the boy's biological father was. Three guards had to rush into the visitor's telephone room to restrain Chester. He was beating his fists on the glass partition and yelling at the top of his lungs.

"Whore! Harlot! I'll kill you! Whore! Whore!" he kept screaming at her, until the guards dragged him out of the room.

Wanda Faye found out later on that they had to give Chester a sedative, and for several days he had to be kept sedated. No, there would be no looking back to Egypt for Wanda Faye.

Nadine was normally reluctant to play the guitar and sing, but tonight, at the end of the sermon, when Brother Linton asked if she would come up and sing Sophie Martin's big hit, "Splendor of Life", she sprang like a rabbit to the front of the church. After grabbing Brother Linton's old Gibson guitar, she briefly tuned it and then stepped to the microphone with a huge smile on her face.

"It's been a long, long time," she said. "Pray for me. This is a song Wanda Faye and I learned as little girls. We've always loved Sophie Martin. I guess if we have heroes other than Jesus our Lord, our mama, or anyone else, it's Sophie Martin. Wanda Faye, come help me sing," she added, looking out to her sister in the audience.

Wanda Faye could have killed her graveyard dead, as Destini would put it, but Nadine was her best friend and her sister. She knew full well, however, that the furtherance of the spirit was not what was on Nadine's mind right now. What was on her mind was the young and handsome preacher with the porcelain veneer caps and the gold Rolex watch, who was smiling from ear to ear and winking at her, as if he had some sort of twitch thing going on with his right eye.

"Mama," Nadine said. "We want to dedicate this to you and to all the Saints of God. Brother Eugene, this goes out to you, as well, and in loving memory of your dear daddy and mama. God rest them."

Nadine plucked the first chords clear and smooth as spring water, and in her lovely Emmy Lou Harris voice, she began to sing.

"As I wander through life, as I reach for the sky, I remember my mama, in the sweet by and by. She loved me and cared for me day after day, and called on the Lord to do as he may."

As Nadine continued, Wanda Faye joined in. Looking out into the audience, she could see tears streaming down her mama's face. She was being consoled by Velma and Mary Lee.

When the girls finished the last verse, the congregation gave them a standing ovation. That's when Wanda Faye spotted someone standing near the front door. It was the face of a man she had held in her mind and her heart since she was a teenager.

Dink had come to church, something he hadn't done in years. It was then that she knew. She knew he had never stopped loving her. As she looked his way and their eyes met, she was certain he knew that she loved him, too.

Chapter 5

When the revival service was over and all the goodbyes had been spoken, Preacher Gene asked Nadine and Wanda Faye to join him for a bite to eat at the Waffle House over in Pittstown. Nadine couldn't say yes fast enough and Wanda Faye only agreed because Nadine kept punching her in the ribs.

While Preacher Gene went to get his car, the two girls went over to the pickup to retrieve their pocketbooks.

"You better remember you're a married woman and that man is a man of God, a holy vessel," Wanda Faye warned Nadine. "I know what's on your mind, girl. You better be careful, is all I'm sayin'."

Nadine simply shrugged and didn't say a word. As they were walking back toward Preacher Gene's late model, white Cadillac Escalade, Wanda Faye spotted Dink across the parking lot and he was staring at her.

"Where you going, Miss Wanda Faye?" he

shouted, and then started walking toward her.

Meanwhile, Nadine didn't skip a beat and continued toward Preacher Gene's car.

"Well, Dink, I guess I'm going with my horny sister over to Pittstown, but I sho' don't want to go," Wanda Faye said when Dink caught up to her.

Dink couldn't help but chuckle at her choice of words.

"What are you doing?" she asked him. "Would you like to come with us? I'd sure like that. If you'll follow us over there, then Preacher Gene won't have to drive us back."

"Well, now, it's been a while since I been asked out on a dinner date by a good lookin' woman," Dink said, smiling. "Yes, ma'am, I'll be glad to accompany you. In fact, I'll accompany both of you," he added, as if he knew what was going through Wanda Faye's mind, that it wouldn't be proper for a man of God to ride off alone with a married woman.

Nadine was just about to get into the preacher's car when Wanda Faye called out to her to come back.

"Hurry up, Nadine! We're ridin' with Dink in his truck!" she yelled.

It was clear from the expression on Nadine's face that she wasn't the least bit happy about Dink's intrusion, but she came back anyway, after telling Preacher Gene they'd meet him over in

Pittstown.

Wanda Faye slid into the cab and sat next to Dink with Nadine climbing in seconds later to sit shotgun. Sitting so close to Dink made Wanda Faye feel awkward at first. He was wearing Aramis cologne, the same brand she had bought for him for his birthday, the day after their little tryst. She recalled buying it from the Lovely Lady store in Pittstown at a bargain price. It pleased her to know that after all these years he was still wearing the same cologne.

"I overheard Mama say Hamp Brayerford offered to put the preacher up at his huntin' lodge while he's in town," Nadine piped up, after sitting quietly and stewing for nearly five minutes.

Hamp Brayerford owned one of the biggest timber farms just north of Seraph Springs and he had recently remodeled his hunting lodge, which entertained guests from around the globe all year round.

"Yeah, I heard Preacher Gene was a huntin' and fishin' enthusiast," Dink said.

"Mama told me the Brayerfords have been long time Episcopalians and they worship idols with incense and such," Wanda Faye interjected. "She also said she was happy when Mr. Hamp agreed to let the preacher stay at his lodge as a kindness to Brother Linton and Sister Velma. When Mr. Hamp lost his mother after a long illness several years ago, it was Mama and Sister

Velma who stayed with her practically around the clock during the last six months of her life. Mr. Hamp couldn't have paid for the kind of care they gave his mama."

"You got that right," Nadine said.

"After she died, Mr. Hamp gave the church a check to completely remodel the fellowship hall at the House of Prayer," Wanda Faye continued. "He also bought a new church van for Mama to transport her Bible Drill soldiers."

"Yep, Mama knew all the Brayerford men drank and played poker, but she never said a word about it," Nadine added. "She never said nothin' bad about Mr. Hamp or any of the Brayerford family, not that I ever heard, anyway."

"Me, either," Wanda Faye said. "Like all of us, he's fallen short of the glory of God, and he knows it. There's never a time when I'm around him that he doesn't grab my hand and ask me to pray for Mama. I believe when we get across the portals of glory, Mr. Hamp will be there."

Dinner at the Huddle House turned out to be more or less uneventful. The girls ordered BLT's and hash browns smothered with onions, the preacher ordered a ham and cheese omelet, and Dink ordered a patty melt with French fries. All of them had coffee to drink.

As they ate, Preacher Gene told the girls how much he loved their singing back at the church.

"Thank you," Nadine said, between bites of her BLT. "Wanda Faye and I have always loved Sophie Martin. We had posters of her in our bedroom when we were growing up, and we scraped together all the money we could from cleaning up the lodge for Mr. Hamp to buy all her albums and tapes. She's our musical hero."

"Yes, she is," Wanda Faye agreed. "Like you said, Preacher Gene, she never looked back to Egypt. She knew what she wanted, and she went for it and accomplished it. You know the Lord had to be with her through all her ups and downs. You got to admire her. She's part of what I call the American Dream. I love her and, of course, folks ask me all the time why I love Margot Smith so much. I tell them that even though she talks about some controversial things, she's an encourager and gives folks hope. She sure helped me when I was living in Georgia and feeling so bad."

"That's a real blessing," Preacher Gene said. "Again, you girls were a blessing tonight, and I can't believe how hospitable and kind the people in Seraph Springs have been. My word, I feel like a visiting dignitary staying out at Mr. Hamp's hunting lodge in all that luxury."

"Preacher Gene, you enjoy your time out

there at Mr. Hamp's place and just be glad them walls can't talk, or you'd be praying all day and half the night," Dink said, laughing.

Preacher Gene laughed along with him and Wanda Faye swore she saw a slight stirring in his poplin suit pants, but she wasn't sure.

After finishing their meal, Dink surprised everyone and picked up the tab. Preacher Gene followed the trio back toward Seraph Springs and honked the horn when he turned off the main highway to head for the hunting lodge.

Fifteen minutes later, Dink dropped the girls off at the church. Wanda Faye lingered a moment beside his window and then chastely kissed him on the cheek.

"Thank you, Dink. You're a doll," she said. "Give me a call, honey. We'll have to do something one day."

Dink smiled at her. "One day soon, Wanda Faye. One day real soon," he said.

As the girls were driving over to Destini's to pick up the children, neither one of them said much. It had been several hours since they'd had a cigarette, so they were both chain-smoking one cigarette after the next, as they listened to a country music radio station out of Barkley.

Conway Twitty and Loretta Lynn were singing, "After the Fire is Gone". When they got to the part that said, "Love is where you find it, when you find no love at home, and there's nothing cold as ashes, after the fire is gone," Wanda Faye looked over at Nadine, who seemed much too moved by the sentiment. She wondered what was going on in her head. She hoped it wasn't something stupid that would cause her to make a fatal mistake.

When they got to Destini's, they found her standing out on the porch waiting for them. Wanda Faye pulled up as close as she could and rolled down the window.

"All the kids are asleep on couches, beds and floor pallets all over the house," Destini quietly told the girls. "Y'all go on home. I'll feed these babies breakfast. You can come tomorrow morning and pick them up."

"Are you sure?" Nadine asked.

"Yes,m, I'm sure. I took 'em all down to the creek right before dark and they had a good bath. They's wearin' some of my big T-shirts now and they's all sleepin' sound."

"What time do you want us to pick them up?" Wanda Faye asked.

"Come on about eight, eight-thirty," Destini said. "I got to get down to the church early for Sunday school. We got the district superintendent coming over from Jacksonville. I already got my ham baked and my hens and dressin' cooked up, and I made three pecan pies and three sweet potato. You girls ought to come out tomorrow. Lots of the spirit will be movin' among the people out there at Mt. Nebo A.M.E. tomorrow. You know y'all always welcome. Folks love to hear y'all pick that guitar and sing."

"Thank you, darling, but we better pass this time," Wanda Faye said. "We've churched plenty this evening, and by the time we get these children home and dressed, it will be time for Mama to come get them and take them to Sunday school. She ain't gonna like it one bit, but we're gonna skip tomorrow. I got a ton of washin' to do. I know the devil's gonna get me for washin' clothes on Sunday, but, honey, the ox is not just in the ditch, he's down in the canyon."

Nadine laughed and explained that her washing machine was broken, and that Wanda Faye was doing the washing for her, as well as doing her own.

"Drying, too," Wanda Faye added. "I sho' am thankful you talked Mr. Hamp into lettin' us do our washin' and dryin' out there at Camp EZ, Destini. With those big, new machines he's got, the work goes much faster. Thank you, too, for gettin' us that part time work helping you out at the parties he has, and cleanin' up out there."

"Baby, think nothin' of it," Destini said. "That ol' man is some kind of card wearin' them ol' Brougham shoes with no socks, and them ol' wore out khakis and work shirts. Mama Tee said his mama, Lillian, had to raise some kinda cane to get him to wear shoes. Ever'body said you could braid briars with the bottoms of his feet, he went without shoes for so long."

Destini had the girls in stitches now and she had to warn them to be quiet or else they'd wake up the children. It didn't stop her from rattling on, though.

"He lives in that ol' run down cabin at the farm with one little window unit and drives them ol' Ford pickups till they's rusted out. Only thing he don't spare money on is food. Mama Tee said she never saw a man eat as much hoppin' john and cornbread in one sittin', and he eats the same thing for supper ever' night of his life. A thick T-bone steak, a green salad with lettuce dressed in mayonnaise, and a baked sweet potato covered with butter. He never drinks iced tea, just water and coffee and, well, y'all know... bourbon. He does like that Old Crow, now, don't he? He takes one big drink when he gets up in the mornin', right after he drinks his coffee and eats his toast, and then has him two big drinks before supper ever' night. That's it. I seen folks try and get him to drink more, but he don't do it. That man is as regular in his habits as a clock. Mama Tee says that's the reason he never married. No woman could put up with that kind of foolishness day in and day out. Well, enough of that. Here's the key. I done called Mr. Hamp and told him y'all was comin' out there. He's leavin' me an envelope on the counter, and y'all bring it back to me. I gotta go up to Sam's in Valdosta Wednesday and shop for the lodge. He's got people comin' to stay out there on Thursday, soon as y'all's preacher leaves. There's some folks from Miami comin' to fish on the river and look at some of his property for turkey huntin'. Some rich Cuban folks, they tell me. I hope they speak good English. I cain't understand all that cacha como say yama them folks speak."

Wanda Faye and Nadine were laughing harder now. Destini had a knack for making folks laugh even when she wasn't trying.

"We'll bring you the envelope, Destini. Anything else you need?" Wanda Faye asked.

With a straight face, she said, "Yeah, if you see Denzel Washington walkin' on the side of the road, and he says he's lonely and needs a good woman, bring him on out here to me."

"Oh, yeah, we'll do that, right after we pick up Tim McGraw for me and Matthew McConaughey for Nadine. Maybe they'll all be together," Wanda Faye said, still laughing.

"If they is, and you let 'em get away, I'm gonna put a whuppin' on you when I see you," Destini said, now laughing herself. "Go on, now. Y'all get outta here. I'm goin' to bed."

Chapter 6

The next morning, Wanda Faye was up at the crack of dawn, and by nine-thirty, when her mama arrived in the Bible Drill van, she had all seven of the children dressed and ready for Sunday school and church.

Each child had to recite their Bible memory verse before getting into the van, which was just one of Miss Jewell's hard and fast rules. The only one exempt at the moment was the baby, Jewell Lee, but even she said, "Jesus loves me" to her grandma before hopping inside. After giving Miss Jewell a perfunctory hug and kiss, one by one the rest of the kids piled into the van.

One major blessing this morning was that Miss Jewell was in such a rush to get the children off to Sunday school that she didn't have time to light into Wanda Faye and Nadine about not going to church today.

She was in her righteous mode when she pulled up, though, and Wanda Faye could hear the McKamey's singing, "God on the Mountain" off a CD inside the van. All the children knew the song by heart, and would even do the little laugh like the lead singer did in the middle of the song. Oftentimes, Miss Jewell would get all of them to sing it for her during a break at the Bible drills.

As soon as Miss Jewell and the kids left, Wanda Faye and Nadine gathered up jumbo-sized, plastic garbage bags full of dirty clothes and put them in the back of the truck, along with laundry detergent, bleach and fabric softener sheets. Then, they drove out to Camp EZ, unloaded everything, and began doing their laundry.

After the first load was put in the commercial-sized washing machine, Nadine and Wanda Faye went exploring through the lodge. They had been inside on several occasions, but only in certain areas, mostly downstairs. Wanda Faye was in awe at the beautiful pine paneling, as well as the huge fireplace and hearth. Destini had told her it was constructed from rock that came from the mountains of North Carolina.

Scattered around the main social room of the lodge were leather couches and chairs. Every single piece of the lavish furniture, the accessories, and even the wall hangings looked like they came from new money. Everything was tastefully done in tartan plaids and camouflage prints.

"This is one of the most beautiful places I've ever seen," Nadine said. "It's not as elegant as the marble and mahogany of Mrs. Hattie Campbell's house in Turpricone, though."

Nadine had helped out at a couple of parties catered by her friend, Rita Rawls, one of which was held at Hattie's home. She had, by far, the most elegant and beautiful home in the county with old family antiques, crystal chandeliers, and lots of silk and satin.

"This place is quietly elegant, though, don't you think, Wanda Faye?" Nadine asked, as she continued to snoop around. "It kinda makes you feel like you're a special friend and can sit down, curl up, and make yourself at home."

"Yes, it does," Wanda Faye agreed, as her thoughts drifted back in time.

She recalled most everything Destini had ever told her about the lodge. When Mr. Hamp built the place, she said it was rumored that it cost him over a million dollars. No expense had been spared, it seemed. A Valdosta contractor and his crew, she told her, ate at the Smokin' Pig in Seraph Springs almost every day while they were building it.

From the plumbing fixtures to the rain gutters, everything, according to the contractor, was tip-top quality. Through the years, Mr. Hamp had collected a lot of fine furnishings, which were now a part of the lodge.

His best friend was Hattie, who was two years younger than him. Her family owned a little less property than the Brayerfords, but it was still a big chunk of geography in the county.

There were only three times a year when Mr. Hamp would dress up in his custom-made, charcoal grey suit, socks and dress shoes; Hattie's Christmas open house, her annual spring cocktail party when her prized heirloom roses first bloomed, and when she'd throw a dinner party for him on his birthday.

At these parties, aside from Mr. Hamp and Hattie, were her sister, Frances Katherine – better known as Nanny to her grandchildren and most everyone else in Campbell County – Judge John Wesson and his wife, and sometimes their slightly flamboyant niece Dee Dee Wilson. Mr. Hamp's nephew, Carl Alvin Brayerford Campbell, and the late Bessie Brayerford Campbell, who had married Mrs. Delbert Frank's husband's brother, Barry, were also regular fixtures at these gatherings.

Hattie's money was acquired through her family, the Wilson's, who owned the largest sawmill in the county, as well as the tobacco warehouses and the feed and seed stores. Her daddy had set up her late husband, Arthur, and his brother by buying them a Ford dealership, or the Ford Store, as her daddy referred to it.

Old man Hamp Brayerford Sr., Mr. Hamp's father, bought a pharmacy for Carl and Bessie after she graduated from Emory University School of Pharmacy. She was one of the first women to do so. Bessie was the industrious one of the couple, making money hand over fist by supplying at least ninety-percent of the pharmaceutical needs to the community.

When Mr. Hamp built Camp EZ, it was Hattie who consulted with the head designer from a top firm in Madison, Georgia, whose designs she loved, and it was she, along with her sister, Nanny, who spent the better part of a year furnishing the lodge with well-chosen pieces. Each one of them coordinated perfectly with the furnishings Mr. Hamp had already bought.

In the beginning, Mr. Hamp told Hattie he didn't care what she spent, within reason, of course, to make the place look stunning.

"But, remember this," he had told her. "I want any son-of-a-bitch in Campbell County to be able to come into my place and feel at ease. I'll be damned if I'm going to have anything that puts folks off. I deal with all kinds of people, and I want something that welcomes the people I've lived around all my life."

Hattie told him if she hadn't known him since they were slobbering babies, she would have sworn he was criticizing her and the way she had decorated her own house. Mr. Hamp denied it, of course, and said he loved her house. He also said he was impressed with all the Savannah fine china and silver that was passed down to her from her mother, which was proudly displayed in her formal dining room.

Destini told Wanda Faye that those few compliments were all Hattie needed and she offered up a kiss on Mr. Hamp's cheek, which, she said, threw him for a loop.

"That's for being you, you ol' sweet thing," Hattie had told him. "Half the county is scared to death of you with your blustering and cussing, but I know you, ol' boy. I've always known you."

Destini said Mr. Hamp got totally flustered and he told Hattie to shut up and have a drink with him.

"You're spending all my damned money, so the least you can do is have a drink with me," he said to her.

And so, over a year's time, Hattie, Nanny and Mr. Hamp worked together five days a week getting the lodge completed to all of their satisfaction.

They ate all their meals together, which were prepared by Destini's mother, Lucy. When Lucy died suddenly, Destini took over. She had been working at the poultry plant at the time and Mr. Hamp bluntly told her to give them notice.

"Whatever they're paying you, I'll double it," he told her. "I gotta have you out here now. Ain't trusting nobody else."

When the lodge was completed, Mr. Hamp decided to throw an open house party to "beat the band". He told everyone he wasn't serving whisky, though.

"Most folks who live around here at least pretend they don't drink," he said. "I ain't gonna make 'em uncomfortable. Now, mind you, I'm gonna have my drink, 'cause I don't give a damn, but I want all the folks around Seraph Springs to come. I've been good to most of 'em, but they been good to me, too."

Hattie called upon the church groups from every black and white church on the south end of Campbell County to provide food for the open house. Mr. Hamp paid for it all and made contributions to all the churches. Destini was the overseer of the preparations, with Wanda Faye, Nadine, their mama and Sister Velma helping out. Meanwhile, Hattie took care of the flower arrangements and table decorations.

Over three-thousand people signed the guest book at Camp EZ that day, and not one went away hungry. They were served fried catfish, barbecued venison and pork, fried chicken, chicken pilau, salads of every description, white acre peas, collards, mustard greens, turnips, hoppin' john, pork backbone and rice, and crab pilau, which was a specialty of the African American community on the south end of the county.

For dessert, there were pecan pies, sweet potato pies, chess pies, banana pudding, and a variety of pound cakes. In the center of the dessert table were a series of gigantic cakes done by a bakery in Jacksonville that were decorated with woodland scenes.

Placed on small tables inside the lodge were huge bowls of salted pecans, trays full of cheese straws and homemade pimiento cheese sandwiches, as well as homemade pepper jelly-covered cream cheese for an assortment of crackers.

Guests were served coffee, soft drinks, lemonade, water or iced tea and, at either end of the large dining room table, ladies from various churches served punch from Hattie's two oversized, silver punch bowls.

The entertainment was provided by local country, bluegrass and gospel groups, all coordinated by Mr. Hamp's nephew, Carl Alvin, who was involved with the local state park, and who was a board member of the big country music park over in Pittstown.

Everyone seemed to be in agreement that the lodge at Camp EZ was not only beautiful, but it was a far cry from the old shack that had been on the property for nearly a century, where millions of catfish had been cleaned and thousands of white-tailed deer had been dressed.

Wanda Faye was following Nadine as she went aimlessly from room to room, humming "Hard Candy Christmas". She had a funny feeling her sister was up to something, but she didn't know what. For now, Wanda Faye decided to just keep an eye on her and make certain she didn't do anything stupid.

Nadine's seemingly aimless path took her upstairs to the master bedroom where Preacher Gene was staying. A plunderer by nature, Wanda Faye watched as Nadine opened the closet and looked inside. There, in a neat row, were his casual clothes, his suits and his dress shirts.

On top of the dresser was a case that contained an assortment of quality silk neckties in various colors, all of them subdued and tasteful. There was also a big bottle of cologne.

"Look at this, Wanda Faye," Nadine said. "Drakkar Noir."

She lifted the bottle to her nose and inhaled the fragrance.

"Good grief, Nadine, don't spray that stuff," Wanda Faye warned her. "You don't want a scent lingering in here. He'll know somebody was snooping around."

Nadine put the bottle back where she found it, but then she opened the top dresser drawer where she found his socks, dark blue, black and brown, all neatly rolled and arranged by color. In the next drawer, she found his underclothes.

"Well, well," she said. "Lookie here. Somebody wears boxers, not briefs, and they're in all different colors."

After opening the other drawers and finding

nothing of interest, she went into the bathroom. It was a man's bathroom, for sure, with black and white tile on the floors and walls, and a huge walk-in shower. A black marble lavatory counter stretched along one entire side of the room. It had two sinks with large camouflaged medicine cabinets perched above them. On the counter were two shaving kits, and they were both zipped tight.

"Nadine, what are you doing?" Wanda Faye asked, getting frustrated with her sister's antics.

"I'm just looking," she said, as she unzipped one of them.

It contained nothing special, just contact lenses, nail clippers, eye drops, toothpaste, a toothbrush, hair gel, antiperspirant, a razor and shaving gel. The second one had hairspray, a bottle of Bayer aspirin, nose spray, after shave balm, and...

When Nadine lifted the after shave balm, Wanda Faye noticed a sly grin on her face. She peeked over her shoulder and gasped when she saw all the condoms. Some were extra thin and others were extra large.

"Looks like somebody came to minister to everyone who has a need in this congregation," Nadine said, smiling. "Praise the Lord."

"Nadine, put all that stuff back, will you, please?" she ordered her. "Come on, now! Get your butt in gear, for gosh sakes. We got enough clothes to wash, dry and fold to fill the children's department at three Wal-Marts, and you're plundering."

"I ain't plundering!" Nadine countered, as she carefully put everything back where she found it.

"Oh, yeah? You're wrong, honey. You're plundering. I know you too well. Come on, will you please? We gotta get this stuff finished. Mama's gonna be through with that Bible drill practice by two-thirty."

"All right, all right," Nadine muttered.

"Go out to the truck and bring us a cold Coke from the cooler and our cigarettes, too," Wanda Faye told her. "Set 'em on that picnic table out back behind the laundry room. I'm fixin' to go dry the first load, and put in another to wash."

"Yes'm, boss lady," Nadine said with a sneer, as Wanda Faye started out of the bathroom.

Wanda Faye turned around in the doorway and asked, "Did you say something?"

"I said, okay, good," Nadine lied. "We need a break," she added, as she watched her sister walk out the bedroom door. "Yep, a break is what I need," she muttered. "A break from Louie and the youngun's. Yes, ma'am, I need to spend the night in the arms of that freckled, angel, preacher man."

Wanda Faye was halfway down the long hallway, so she wasn't privy to Nadine's declaration of intended infidelity.

Chapter 7

The view from Nadine's eyes

Before Nadine went to fetch the Cokes and Marlboros, she took a detour into the kitchen, talking quietly to herself as she devised her plan.

"It took the Lord seven days to make the world," she said. "I hope to make Preacher Gene in less than an hour after slipping back out here tonight."

Without further ado, and after making certain no one was watching her, she grabbed the spare house key from a big rack of keys on the wall, which were all clearly marked. Then, she jotted down the alarm code on the inside of her wrist.

"Before midnight, Preacher Gene, you'll be callin' out, oh, Jesus, oh, God, but you won't be praying," she said, smiling from ear to ear as she pranced out of the kitchen.

That night, Nadine fixed Louie and the children their usual Sunday night meal, which they referred to as their morning supper, because it was pancakes and sausage. After most of the dinner dishes were washed, dried and put away, Nadine made sure all the children got their baths, brushed their teeth and said their prayers, and then she tucked each one of them in for the night.

Next, it was off to take care of Louie. She rubbed his back with heat balm, as she'd been doing ever since he hurt himself on the job. He swore it did his back some good and made him feel better. After the rubdown, she gave him his nightly muscle relaxer, his pain pill, and then turned on his heating pad and placed it on his back.

As she tidied up the last of the pots and pans from supper, she heard Louie begin to snore. The children had been asleep for a good hour now. It seemed they were dead tired from the drill Miss Jewell put them through at church.

"I know I shouldn't be doing this, but..." Nadine said.

Trying to be as quiet as she could, she tiptoed into the bedroom, where a fragranced night light beside the bed offered just enough illumination for her to see.

She continued over to the closet and inched open the door, making sure it didn't creak or squeak. She reached inside and gently pulled a low-cut, white silk blouse off its hanger where she had strategically placed it earlier in the evening. After quickly removing her long-sleeved cotton shirt, she slipped the blouse on over her head, and then admired her reflection in the mirror that was nailed to the inside of the closet door. It showed off her ample bosom quite nicely, she thought.

"Not bad," she said, and then she cupped her hand over her mouth, afraid Louie may have heard her.

He was fast asleep, though, and still snoring as loud and as repetitiously as one of her uncle's old buzz saws. He would be out cold until at least five in the morning when the medication wore off and she knew it. It had been that way forever and a day.

Next, she grabbed the shortest denim skirt she owned and a pair of gold sandals. Dee Dee Wilson had given them to her as a thank you gift a few years ago after she helped her decorate her house for a big Christmas party she was throwing.

Once she had all she needed from the closet, Nadine tiptoed back out of the bedroom and hurried down the hall to the bathroom. As soon as she finished getting dressed, she touched up her makeup and then brushed her hair before pulling it back into a ponytail.

As she assessed herself in the bathroom mirror, she thought she looked damned good.

"Oops, almost forgot," she said.

She grabbed the bottle of Chanel Number Five cologne from the medicine chest that Wanda Faye had given her for her birthday nearly three years ago. There was barely enough liquid left in the bottle to do any good, but she managed to lightly spritz herself in all the pertinent places before the bottle emptied itself out.

Within seconds, she was easing out the front door with the stealth of a feline in heat. She pushed the old Chevy pickup to the end of the drive, then hopped in, cranked it, and was on her way. As much as she wanted a cigarette, and as much as she needed one right now to calm her nerves, she didn't light up.

"You never know, Preacher Gene may get turned off if he smells cigarette smoke on me," she said, but it didn't stop the nagging, addictive urge from driving her crazy.

As she pulled off the paved highway and veered onto the long dirt road to Camp EZ, she turned off her headlights. She had been down this road enough times that she felt confident she could avoid all the bumps, dips and potholes. She made sure to re-inventory them in her brain earlier today when she and Wanda Faye came to do the laundry.

As she pulled into the front yard of the camp, she turned off the engine and waited until the truck stopped on its own, as it gently butted up against a small pile of rocks. When she stepped out, she spotted Preacher Gene's car parked underneath the outdoor carport by the front of the lodge. He had evidently gone through the front door when he arrived, rather than park in the four-car garage at the back of the lodge that was reserved for guests.

She could see a dim light burning in the foyer from a large brass lamp that was sitting on the hall table. There was also a bright light coming from the master bedroom suite where Preacher Gene was staying.

As slick as a two bit thief, she unlocked the door, slipped inside, and hurriedly punched in the alarm security code.

"Phew!" she said under her breath. "Well, I'm in. Now, what?" she thought, as she quickly scanned the area to be sure no one was lurking around.

As she slowly made her way across the great room and up the steps to the hall that led to the bedroom suites, her heart was pounding so hard she thought for certain she was going to have a heart attack before she could consummate the deed.

There were seven bedroom suites at the lodge. Each one contained its own small sitting room and bathroom. Two of them were designed for the ladies with a small dressing room in more feminine décor. All the rooms had antique chaise lounges covered in a mauve silk material.

She had memorized the layout of the house, the same way she did for the long, dirt road that led to the lodge. She even knew which floorboards might creak and squeak. The photographic memory that she'd been blessed with since childhood seemed to be holding its own.

She proceeded with care down the darkened hallway, past the hunting prints, and the deer and bear heads that lined the walls.

"This is a little creepy," she thought, as she tried to stay in the center of the walkway, well away from the pointy antlers jutting out from the stuffed heads.

As she rounded the corner and entered the corridor that led to the master suite, she heard what sounded like moaning... and then someone began to scream. It was a muffled tone, but it was definitely screaming she was hearing.

She stopped dead in her tracks. For a moment, she thought Preacher Gene might be in some kind of distress. When the noise quieted down, she quickened her pace and rushed to his bedroom door.

Something in her gut told her not to barge right in like a rookie cop hoping to make a name for himself in the local paper by catching a thief red-handed.

Instead, she quietly turned the knob and cracked the door open just far enough so she could peek inside. The smell of burning incense wafted up her nostrils and for a brief moment she thought she might find Preacher Gene lying prone on the bed in a silk robe, puffing on a Cuban cigar, as he awaited her arrival.

As she opened the door a bit farther, she noticed the room was lit up like a brothel on Christmas Eve, with several multi-colored lamps throughout the expansive suite. All the lamp bases were made out of deer antlers, but each one had a different colored shade with matching colored light bulbs. Her loins began to stir from all the romantic suspense of this wild adventure and she smiled ever so slightly.

As her eyes scanned the room from one end to the other searching for the bed, she almost did have a heart attack. Right there in front of her, not twenty feet away with his backside staring her in the face, was Preacher Gene, naked as the day he was born. He was standing beside the bed, and on his knees in front of him, was the one and only Carl Alvin Campbell... in the flesh!

She watched as Preacher Gene lifted Carl Alvin off the floor, kissed him dead on the mouth while in a long embrace, and then he ripped off his shirt and threw him onto the bed in one fell swoop. The pants came off next and then a pair of white briefs went flying through the air over toward where Nadine was huddled in the doorway.

She was in such a state of shock she could

hardly turn away, but she knew she had to before she hurled her pancakes and sausages all over the plush, red carpet. She quickly shut the door and leaned against the doorjamb like a tin soldier, unable to move as she tried to digest what she had just witnessed.

From inside the room, she could hear the moans of sexual satisfaction coming out of the mouths of both Preacher Gene and Carl Alvin. It was almost too much for her to fathom. She didn't know whether to laugh or cry. She didn't know if she was going to be sick or whether she should feel exhilarated at having just witnessed firsthand what really goes on behind some folks' closed doors.

One thing was for certain. She wouldn't be cheating on Louie this evening. Perhaps, after tonight, she would never even entertain the thought of cheating on her husband... ever again.

Her mind started racing with all kinds of thoughts. For one, she was pissed off that her plan had failed, even though it was probably for the best. For another, she knew she had to get out of there quickly before one or both of the men decided to come out of the bedroom and go outside for a cigarette, which she had been Jonesing for ever since she left her house.

Before leaving the dreadful scene behind her, never to think of again, she hoped, she decided she would make her presence known by leaving

Carl Alvin a note on the windshield of his car.

She hurried downstairs and went into the laundry room. There was a pad of paper and a pen on the small counter by the telephone, which she had noticed was there earlier in the day. She wrote the following:

July 12, 2009

Dear Carl Alvin,

I always liked you. I still do. I never have paid no mind to the bad things people said about you. I seen Preacher Gene and you having a good time tonight. Seems like y'all was enjoying it, too. I ain't tryin to hold you up, Carl Alvin, but I want you to talk to your cousin, Hugh Jr., and get my case finished with. You been workin' on it now for over a year. My children need to go to the dentist and so do I.

I ain't gonna tell a soul in the world what I seen, not even Wanda Faye. Me and you are friends, and we always will be. Your friend, Nadine.

The first thing she noticed when she walked out the front door was Carl Alvin's Cadillac. He was parked right beside Preacher Gene's Cadillac, which was one detail that failed to register in her brain when she first arrived.

After she placed the note under the driver's side windshield wiper of Carl's car, she hurried over to her truck. Just as she was about to pull out to leave, she remembered something.

"Dammit! I forgot to set the alarm!" she yelled, and she shut off the engine.

Without further ado, and not wanting to hang around any longer than was necessary, she ran back inside, punched in the alarm code, and then quietly shut the door behind her before running back to her truck.

As she was pulling away, with a cigarette in one hand and her lighter in the other, she glanced in the rearview mirror and spotted both Preacher Gene and Carl Alvin coming out the door. They both seemed to be glowing in the darkness, or maybe it was just her imagination. At this point, she wasn't sure of much of anything.

When she got far enough away from the lodge, she flipped on the headlights and high-tailed it home as fast as she could.

❧❧❧❧❧❧❧❧❧❧

Nadine never did receive a telephone call from Carl Alvin, but Louie did the following day. Two weeks later, they got a check from Hugh Campbell's law firm for over two-hundred-thousand dollars, three times the amount Nadine thought they would get. Hugh didn't charge a dime for his legal services, either. Louie was overjoyed and all Nadine could do was smile.

"The Lord moves in mysterious ways," she later told Louie.

With the money from the lawsuit, Nadine set about doing the things she needed to have done. She didn't go crazy with spending, though. She told Louie there wouldn't be a new car or truck out of the deal. Instead, Mr. Hamp sold her a large van that had been used by the hunting lodge. It only had thirty-five-thousand miles on it and there was enough room inside for all the children and then some. With the more than fair price he offered her, she jumped on the deal.

Then, she paid off their mobile home, had the entire place insulated, added central heating and air conditioning, and had all new energy-efficient windows installed. She and all the children also had a field day at the dentist getting their teeth cleaned, cavities filled, and she even splurged on a couple of gold caps for her lower back molars.

A few weeks later, Nadine, Wanda Faye and Destini loaded up all the kids and took them to the big water and amusement park near Valdosta. They had always wanted to go, but they had never been able to afford it. It was an enjoyable day for everyone, especially the adults, as they watched the children splash around in the water and have a big ol' time.

The best part was when the children screamed with laughter, as they watched their mamas come flip-flopping down the tall water slide. It was a wonderful day.

Wanda Faye never asked for one thing from her sister and Nadine knew she wouldn't. It was just the way Wanda Faye was. In truth, though, it had always been Wanda Faye who had helped her the most throughout the years.

One afternoon before Bible school let out, Nadine drove out to Camp EZ where Destini was working, just to talk to her for a few minutes. When she pulled up to the lodge, she saw her out front sweeping the concrete walkway that led to the front door. Destini smiled at her and offered her usual big wave of welcome.

Destini invited her up to sit for a spell on the screened porch. She brought out a couple of ash trays, two big glasses of sweet iced tea with lemon, and a small platter containing slices of her "killer" pound cake.

Without Nadine having to say a word, Destini took the lead after taking a drag from her Newport.

She looked her friend in the eyes, and said, "I been thinking, and I sho' is glad we've been friends all these years, but I'm gonna tell you something," Destini began. "Your sister still has an aching heart. Yes'm, for all her happiness in being home, and all the love she gives all of us and all these churrin, that heart still ain't whole. She's still searchin' and lookin'."

"I know," Nadine said, nodding her head.

"Wanda Faye was one of the smartest girls in our class at school. She sho' was. She was so much smarter than some of them who thought they was so high. How you think she passed that GED test without ever pickin' up a book to study? If you wanna do something for that gal, send her over to the Vo-Tech in Barkley, to that nurse assistant training program. She's always talking 'bout that and working with ol' peoples. Pay for her to go over there. My oldest sister, Mae, she finished over there, and she could help her with everything."

"Destini, how the hell did you get so smart? All our lives, I seen you walk around like you ain't thinking one thing in the world, and then pow! You surprise everybody!"

"Well," Destini said, and then she paused to take a sip of her tea. "I think lots about that little picture with the sayin' on it that Mr. Hamp has up in his office. It's a picture of an owl and on it is written, 'A wise old owl sat in an oak, the more he heard, the less he spoke, the less he spoke, the more he heard.' Why can't we be like that wise bird, Nadine?" she asked.

Nadine simply shook her head and then it struck her like a ton of bricks, as she took Destini's words to heart.

"I'll do it, Destini, but how's she goin' to work at the poultry plant and go to school?"

Destini's face brightened.

"She ain't got to work at the plant no more."

"What do you mean?"

"Well, Miss Nadine, I done talked to Mr. Hamp. With the fall season about to start and all them big shots coming out here from ever'where, I'm gonna need another set of hands, 'specially at night, when I have to serve cocktails and dinner. Mr. Hamp said he'd be glad to hire Wanda Faye, 'specially when I told him she was goin' to nursin' school. He said he was glad to help her any way he could."

"Well," said Nadine. "You put some thought into this, I do declare."

With that, Nadine rose from her chair and went over to hug her old friend.

"You ain't goin' funny on me, is you girl?" Destini asked, laughing.

"Hell, no!" Nadine shouted. "And if I was, it wouldn't be over you! I just love ya, girl. I don't say it enough, but I do, I love you."

"I love you, too, baby. That won't never change. There's two more things I'm gonna tell you. You may not wanna hear it, but I'm gonna say it. It's about your mama."

"Mama?" Nadine gasped. "What about her?"

"Now, I know Miss Jewell can get on your last nerve with all that prayin' and testifyin', but listen to me. Y'all wouldn't had a roof over your head if it hadn't been for your mama fightin' your daddy like a dog. He dreaded her and that's the reason he didn't drink ever'thin' up he made. Miss Jewell ain't never asked one thing of y'all, except to go to church and go to them Bible drills, but the one thing she loves is that little, funny-haired evangelist, Lenny Lister."

"Oh, don't you know it?" Nadine chimed in.

"Her and Sister Velma watch that man on television, and they even got enough of his prayer cloths that they made a prayer quilt by quiltin' them pieces together. They put that quilt over peoples down at the church when they at the altar and in the spirit. You seen 'em do it."

"Yes, I have," Nadine said.

"That man is next to Jesus to them, and he's takin' a group of folks to the Holy Land. It'll cost you several thousand dollars to send your mama and Sister Velma over there, but I think you ought to do it and surprise 'em with it at the homecoming at the House of Prayer. The trip goes in October durin' the Feast of Tabernacles, and Mr. Hamp said he'd get their passports done for them. He said he has a connection in Washington that'd get them here in five days."

"My, God, Destini. You are so right. I will. I'll do that for Mama and Sister Velma. Maybe it'll make Mama feel better about ever'thin' we've put her through. I do love her, but she can be a pistol ball sometimes."

"More than a pistol ball, honey," Destini said. "Yer mama is the bomb, and I don't mean that in no particular complimentary way. Mama Tee always say, if Miss Jewell set her head on somethin', only Jesus hisself can turn her from it, and they ain't never been a lazy bone in her body."

"You got that right," Nadine said in agreement.

"You could always eat off that floor at y'alls house, and nobody had prettier clothes than you and Wanda Faye, and she made ever' one of 'em. Made me some dresses, too. Your mama's a good woman. She just ain't playing by nobody's rules but hers and what she believes about that Bible."

"Yep, that's Mama, all right," Nadine said, smiling as she took another drag off her cigarette.

Chapter 8

After Nadine's visit with Destini, she zipped over to the church to pick up the children. Then, she drove everyone to Wanda Faye's apartment.

Wanda Faye was standing at the ironing board in the kitchen, aimlessly pressing the never-ending number of clothes for all the children, including Nadine's kids.

Even though Wanda Faye knew Nadine would have been just as happy if she had simply hung the clothes up after they were dried, and then send the kids off to school, wrinkles and all, Wanda Faye was having none of that. Just like their mama, she insisted that everything be ironed just so.

The children immediately ran off to the little playground in the apartment complex, which gave Nadine a few minutes alone to talk with her sister.

"Wanda Faye," Nadine started, "I done somethin' for you. I hope you ain't gonna be mad with me."

"Oh, Lord," Wanda Faye replied, rolling her eyes. "What have you done this time? Have you enrolled me in one of them courses through a magazine to develop bigger bosoms? I don't need bigger bosoms, Nadine."

"No, it ain't nothin' like that. I went over to the Vo-Tech and I paid the principal over there for your full nurse's assistant program."

Wanda Faye was visibly stunned and she stopped ironing. For a moment or two, she said nothing. When she found her voice, she turned to Nadine.

"Say that again."

"I said you are paid up to make a nurse," Nadine told her.

Wanda Faye very seldom broke down in tears, but the waterworks began to flow down her cheeks now, and she dropped to her chair sobbing uncontrollably. Nadine seemed completely surprised at her reaction.

"Are you mad with me, Wanda Faye?" she asked.

"No, you crazy thing. I'm happy. You and Destini cooked this up, didn't you? You ain't done this on your own. Destini's the one who knows about me watching Margot Smith and loving that series she had about reaching your potential. I confided to her about my dreams of being a nurse."

"Well, sister, this dream's come true," Nadine said. "I know you're thinking about the children and your job, but don't, and don't worry 'bout me. I put enough aside, I ain't gonna have to work for at least a year, and with Louie's Social Security disability that Carl Alvin's gettin' for him, we'll be all right for a good while."

When Nadine told her Destini talked with Mr. Hamp about her working at the lodge at nights, Wanda Faye's eyes widened with delight.

"You'll have to be out there ever' night except Sundays, from six to eleven or twelve, but he's gonna pay you more'n you're makin' over there at Freeman Fryer's, and you can go to school during the day," Nadine told her.

Wanda Faye hugged her sister so tight she yelped, and then she thanked her over and over again.

"You're an angel, you bad thing," she told Nadine. "I never said any different. You can be aggravatin', but you know I've always loved you more than anything or anyone in the world, except my babies. Goodness, no more chicken pluckin'. I love you so much, Nadine."

Now it was Nadine who was dabbing at her eyes, which were filled with tears.

"Stop it, you silly bitch, you're gonna make me ruin my eye makeup, and I was hoping to turn Louie on tonight," Nadine said. "Destini helped me with it, and we tried to get that sultry movie star look. What do you think?"

"Y'all didn't do so bad," Wanda Faye said. "You look beautiful."

"One other thing," Nadine said. "I'm sending Mama and Sister Velma to the Holy Land with Lenny Lister. I also bought Mama Tee one of them new recliners with the button that lets you up and down. Destini said when they delivered it, she complained some, but that she's seen her working that chair, and now she loves it. Even though she can't see, I special-ordered that chair in bright, fire engine red, her favorite color."

"Oh, my word," Wanda Faye said. "You are somethin' else, girl."

"Well, Wanda Faye, get your little white uniforms ready, Miss Florence Nightingale, because soon you're gonna be a nurse. You might even be able to play doctor with Dink."

With that, both girls laughed and laughed until their bellies hurt. Just then, the children came barreling through the door, screaming it was time for a snack.

After the kids ran back outside with their cookies, crackers and iced tea, it was time for Margot Smith's television program, so the two girls retreated to the living room. As always, Wanda Faye's eyes were glued to the set.

"Today could be the day your dreams come true," Margot said, as the show began.

Wanda Faye was nodding her head up and

down, while Nadine sat watching her and the glow of happiness that was spreading across her face.

"If you only knew, Miss Margot. If you only knew," Wanda Faye said, and then she turned and kissed her sister on the cheek.

Chapter 9

The next several weeks, which led through the end of August and the beginning of September, were a flurry of activity for Nadine, Wanda Faye, and their children.

It was time for school to start and all seven of the children had just been enrolled for another year. A full two days was spent in Gainesville buying school clothes and supplies. Wanda Faye insisted they go down when the stores advertised the "tax free" days given by the Governor of Florida. With all the children, and buying clothes and shoes for each one of them, being able to save seven or eight per cent on sales tax was a huge savings for them.

Destini went with the girls, and they stayed overnight with Destini's brother, Duke, and his wife, Essie, who had a huge home on a lake just outside the city limits of Gainesville. Duke was a police officer for the University of Florida, and Essie had worked for years in the registrar's office. Both of them were close to retirement, and since their only son, Duke Jr., was now working on Wall Street up in New York City, the empty-nesters were happy for the company.

Essie and Duke both took a couple of vacation days, so they could thoroughly enjoy the visit. While Wanda Faye, Nadine, Destini and Essie took the girls shopping, Duke entertained the boys by taking them out fishing on the lake in his boat. He also took them to Payne's Prairie State Park and to the movies.

Since their mothers had the boys' clothing sizes, and knew what they'd like, there was nothing left to do, except to take them shopping for new shoes. Duke offered to do so, as well as see to it they got haircuts.

Essie was the chairperson for planning all the big dinners at her church, and she had everything organized and ready for the eight children who descended upon her house. She and Duke managed them without missing a beat, and there was not one cross word spoken the entire time they were there.

The Monday after shopping for school clothes, Wanda Faye registered for her classes at the Vo-Tech in Barkley. She was nervous and excited at the same time, and she tried her best to take down every word the instructor said at orientation. She was determined to be a good student and to make a good nurse.

The nursing instructor, Mrs. Susan Roberts,

was a grandmotherly type woman with the most beautiful white hair Wanda Faye had ever seen. She had a kind face and light green eyes that twinkled.

Mrs. Roberts told them during orientation that she started as a nurse's assistant in a military hospital during the Viet Nam War, and that after losing her first husband in that war, she went back to school and became an R.N. She had worked as a private care nurse in a nursing home, and in large veterans hospitals across the nation.

Her Master's thesis, which she had completed at a college in New England, had been on the care of the terminally ill. It was evident to Wanda Faye that the woman knew her stuff. She was no nonsense, thorough, and she told all the students from the get-go that she would not tolerate foolishness, since the lives of human beings would be placed in their hands, assuming they were worthy and serious about becoming a nurse's assistant.

Each day, Monday through Friday, Wanda Faye left the house before her children were out of bed, getting to the school by seven-thirty. At two-thirty in the afternoon, she would rush home to greet her children when they came in from school. She got to spend a few precious minutes with them before leaving the house a little after four o'clock to go to work at Camp EZ. Her first chore would be helping Destini get ready for cocktail hour for the guests, and then they would prepare the evening meal.

She was happy to learn, not for Mr. Hamp's sake, but for her own, that for the months of August, September, and the first week in October, nobody was scheduled for the lodge on Sunday nights, Mondays and Tuesdays. This gave her more time to be with her children and more time to study.

Not one time during all that time was she ever late for work or school. Her assignments were done, and she stayed at Camp EZ until the last dish was washed and the last ash tray was emptied.

Dink had taken to coming by on Sunday evenings to visit her. He started out calling her before coming by to make sure she was alone, but now he was coming over whether the children were there or not. If they were there, he turned into as big a child as them, playing video games, watching silly movies, and taking them out to the fast food restaurant at the Interstate for cheeseburgers.

When the kids weren't around, Dink spent his time talking to Wanda Faye over endless cups of coffee about his work at the garage, her nurse's schooling, and his hopes to go to work for a big, new trucker transport line into which Mr. Hamp had bought an interest.

During the first couple of weeks Dink came to

visit, he never did more than kiss her on the cheek goodbye, and she wondered if he had any interest in her at all, other than just being a friend. She thought maybe she had read the signals wrong that night of the revival service.

Right before her twenty-fifth birthday, toward the end of September, Dink called her and asked if he could take her out for supper on the night of her birthday. Since it fell on a Monday, and Camp EZ didn't have any guests, she agreed.

When he picked her up, he gave her a bouquet of pink roses he had bought at a local grocery store. There were so many of them and they were so pretty that she placed them in the only large vase she had. It was one that held roses that Destini and Nadine bought for her for Valentine's Day, the first year she came home from Georgia.

That night, Dink took her over to a steak and seafood restaurant that she said she liked in Barkley. She had only been there a couple of times, but she really enjoyed it. The restaurant was located in a restored service station and was decorated with all kinds of football memorabilia, old fishing lures, antique bottles, and all sorts of conversational items.

After a delicious shrimp dinner with all the trimmings, she and Dink took an alternative route home to Seraph Springs. Wanda Faye had just about given up smoking since she started nursing school, as Mrs. Roberts told her she ought to try, so that she could set a good, healthy example for her patients.

As they were driving along, the nicotine urge got the better of her and so she lit one up. It was the first one she'd smoked all evening. After taking a long drag, she leaned over and turned the radio down, and then turned toward Dink.

"What are you doin'?" she asked him.

"What do you mean, Wanda Faye? I'm drivin' you home. Somethin' wrong? You didn't like your supper?" he asked her.

"No, Dink, the supper was very nice, the roses were very nice, and you have been very nice to me and my children. My question, once again, is what are you doin', Dink?"

"I like you Wanda Faye," he said. "I like the children. I like you a whole lot. Well, you know what I mean."

"No, I don't know what you mean, but I want to tell you what I mean," she said. "I love you, Dink. I always have. I'm just gonna tell you, since we was in sixth grade at the elementary school, I never loved nobody else but you. I married Chester because you wasn't old enough to marry. Hell, I wasn't old enough, either, but all during that time, Dink, I loved you. Now, I'm going to school, and I'm going to be a good nurse, and I'm going to continue to be a good mama and set a good example for my children."

"I have no doubt you will," Dink said.

"Anyway, Dink, if you don't love me and my children, then don't come around no more. But... if you're going to stay around, you can sleep with me, at your house or mine, when the children aren't around. There won't be no sleepin' over when my children are there, and Dink, if you want to stick around, there won't be no game playin', 'cause I've seen enough games for a lifetime. I don't have time for them, Dink. So, once again, what are you doin'?"

Dink had a pallid look about him. Wanda Faye thought if someone had cut his jugular vein, he wouldn't have bled a drop. For a solid minute that seemed to her like an eternity, he said absolutely nothing. She turned away and kept puffing on her cigarette, waiting for him to say something... anything. Then, he suddenly jerked the truck over to the side of the road and cut off the engine.

As the sounds of silence enveloped them, Dink cleared his throat and turned to look directly into her eyes.

"Wanda Faye Lee Easley, will you marry me?"

For a few seconds, it seemed everything had gone all fuzzy. Wanda Faye felt numb and tingly all over.

"What did you say, Dink?" she asked him, and then had the good sense to toss her cigarette butt out the window before the ashes fell onto her lap.

"I said... will you marry me?"

"Dink, are you crazy? You know I'm in school, and you know I got four children under the age of ten. You know how I'm workin' right now. Are you on some kind of medication?"

"Wanda Faye, I ain't askin' again. I been wantin' to ask you for over ten years. I asked one other time, and the whole time I was with my ex wife, all I ever thought about was you. I won't say this but one time Wanda Faye, cause I ain't one to run around sayin' it over and over again. People say it too much these days, but I love you, Wanda Faye. I've always loved you, and I always will. I will love your children just like they was mine, and I'll be good to them. I'll be good to you. So, again, Wanda Faye, will you marry me?"

For years, in the deep the recesses of her brain, there were cobwebs and vapors caused by fear, self-doubt, and a lack of self-confidence. Right now, though, it was as if the fog had lifted. It was shining bright like the golden, yellow sun inside her head for the first time in her adult life. She felt completely clear, uncluttered and, most importantly, completely content.

"This must be what Miss Margot was referring to when she talked about people feeling happy. This is what happy feels like," she thought.

With a deliberate twist of her body toward Dink, she looked into his eyes and said as clearly as she could, "Yes, Mr. Drayfuss Lowell, I will... I will marry you."

Dink pulled her to him and then reached in his pocket. What he pulled out was a diamond eternity ring, and the stones weren't little ones, either. They wrapped all the way around a platinum band. Even though she had seen the huge diamonds worn by Hattie Campbell, Dee Dee Wilson, and all of Mr. Hamp's timber crowd, she'd never seen a more beautiful ring in her life because this one was hers.

Dink slipped the ring on her finger and then kissed her deeply.

"Now, Wanda Faye, I hope we ain't got to wait till we're married to consummate things, and I hope you don't mind that I bought that ring at Bubba's Pawn Shop right after I saw you at the Blue Hole."

"Dink, I don't care if you bought the ring from Lucifer himself," she said. "One more thing, baby. If you ain't never been to heaven, honey, you'll be goin' there tonight."

Dink smiled a big, knowing smile, kissed her full on the mouth, and then he cranked up the engine and pulled back onto the highway. He and Wanda Faye sat shoulder to shoulder and thigh to thigh in the cab of the truck as they continued on their way, and then he reached over and gently took hold of her hand.

At that instant, Patsy Cline's melodic voice began to stream from the radio's speakers on either side of them. As she sang one of her biggest hits, “Sweet Dreams”, Dink drove a little faster than usual toward his place in Seraph Springs.

That night, among tangled sheets, sweet perspiration, moans of delight and whispered “I love you’s,”, Wanda Faye and Dink made passionate love to one another. Both of them had found in each other’s arms, kisses, touches and caresses, not only the meaning of happiness, but more importantly, the meaning of true love.

Chapter 10

The day after Dink's proposal, Wanda Faye called a family meeting at her mother's house, which included Destini and Bunnye. With Dink by her side, she announced the happy news. It didn't seem to surprise anyone, except maybe her mother, although, even she seemed overwhelmingly pleased about the upcoming nuptials. Miss Jewell hugged them both and offered her heartiest congratulations.

"My only request and my heart's desire is to see you married right here in your hometown at the House of Prayer," Miss Jewell told her daughter. "I ain't never had neither of my girls married here in the home church and I think it's about time."

Miss Jewell offered to call Brother Linton and Sister Velma to give them the good news, and she asked Wanda Faye and Dink to make certain to be in church on Sunday, so they could speak with Brother Linton about arranging a pre-marital counseling session. The newly-engaged couple were more than eager to comply with her request. They also agreed to put the wedding off until after the October homecoming event at the church.

"I always imagined a spring wedding with light pink, yellow, lavender and light blue as my colors, but I ain't waitin' till spring to marry," Wanda Faye said, shaking her head.

Dink was in agreement and said, "The sooner the better."

As the conversation turned to wedding preparations, Nadine and Destini seemed as caught up in the exciting plans as Wanda Faye. Nadine told her it didn't matter if she married on Christmas or in the dead of winter because she was the bride, and she could have a spring wedding anytime of the year, no matter what anybody said.

"You can have a wedding with all the spring, pastel colors you want," Nadine said. "You just leave it to me and Destini."

Right after they decided on a wedding date for the Saturday before Thanksgiving, Miss Jewell was on the phone with Sister Velma making sure the church and fellowship hall would be available on that date.

"We're all set," Miss Jewell said, smiling as she hung up the phone.

The next morning, Nadine went over to Wanda Faye's apartment to continue discussing wedding plans. Even though Nadine wanted to go whole hog crazy and spend a lot of money on the nuptials, Wanda Faye wouldn't allow it.

"No," she told Nadine. "Me and Dink ain't puttin' on a show for nobody. I just want a small, intimate weddin' with you, Louie, all the children, yours and mine, Mama, Destini, Bunnye, Mama Tee, Duke and Essie, Brother Linton and Sister Velma, sweet little Jerri Faye, Mr. Hamp, Carl Alvin, Miss Hattie, Miss Nanny, Judge and Mrs. Wesson, Dee Dee, Mrs. Roberts, all of Dink's brothers and their wives, and my new friend from the Vo-Tech, Lollie Sears."

Nadine raised her eyes. "Who's Lollie Sears?" she asked. "That name sounds familiar."

"You remember... ol' lady Bertha Sears? She lived way out on the Bailey Route near the Georgia line. Well, she lived in that old shotgun house up there, and Mr. Hamp always rented a section of her land for huntin' because it joined with his. She was kin somehow to Mr. Hamp's mama, Miss Lillian."

"Oh, yeah, I do remember her," Nadine said. "She always raised them tiny, white acre peas. Ever' year, she'd call Mama, and her and Mama Tee and Sister Velma would go out there and pick for several days. Then, they'd all shell together."

"Yep, that's the lady I'm talkin' about," Wanda Faye said.

"I remember during winter, the church ladies would go out there and quilt with the old woman," Nadine continued. "Mama always said Sister Bertha wasn't regular in church attendance, but she could shout down any of 'em when the spirit hit her."

"Oh, don't you know it?" Wanda Faye said in agreement.

"Mama said Sister Bertha was a true believer, and when she died, she left the church enough money to have the whole building and the fellowship hall re-roofed," Nadine went on. "She didn't have no church funeral, just a graveside service. Mama said it was surprising to see all the quality folks who came to the cemetery."

"Well, Lollie is Miss Bertha's granddaughter, her only son's daughter, and she's going to the cosmetology school at the Vo-Tech," Wanda Faye explained. "She has her sights set on being a hairdresser. You know her aunt owns that big beauty shop up in Turpricone."

"Really?" Nadine asked.

"Yep, it's her mama's baby sister, the one who moved here from Mississippi. She was one of them menopause babies, so she's a lot younger than you might expect. She bought Betty's Beauty Box. Her real name is Eileen, but most everyone calls her Miss Sissy. Lollie says she's a pretty thing with platinum blonde hair and her makeup is always done up to the teeth. They say when she lived out there in Jackson, Mississippi, that she did the hair of all the big wigs in the state, even the governor's wife. Now, she's got all the big wigs in Turpricone as clients."

Nadine turned quiet as she rummaged through her purse and Wanda Faye wondered what she was searching for.

"Here it is," Nadine said, and she pulled out a business card. "I knew I had it. Dee Dee gave this to me out at Camp EZ last week when they had that big party with all them folks from South Dakota."

"Let me see," Wanda Faye said, and Nadine handed her the card.

"Me and her was sittin' over there laughin' and makin' fun of one girl who was kin to that bunch who works with Carl Alvin in Turpricone. Big gal, Jean, I think her name was. Them South Dakota folks was her brothers, and let me tell you, they all got steamed during the cocktail hour. Jean was tryin' to play "Suwannee River" on the piano and sing for them, but she was slurrin' so bad, you couldn't half understand her."

"Oh, my goodness," Wanda Faye said, stifling a laugh.

"Dee Dee told me Carl Alvin was supposedly involved with her, because them brothers is all hoity-toity out there in the Midwest in some big lumber company," Nadine went on. "Anyhow, we was laughin' how them folks talked and all when Dee Dee gave me this card. She told me if ever me and you wanted to go for a day of beauty, this was the place to go."

Wanda Faye looked at the card again. On it, written in gold lettering, was:

Betty's Beauty Box
110 Campbell Avenue, Turpricone, Florida
Eileen "Miss Sissy" Paquette
Owner and Operator

Underneath, in quotation marks, written in beautiful gold calligraphy, was *"Beauty Has No Pain"*.

Wanda Faye related to Nadine how she and Lollie ate lunch together almost every day and had become good friends.

"She's a little younger than me and she ain't never been married, but she's datin' a young man who's a pharmacist up in Valdosta," Wanda Faye said. "His name's Jimmy McRae. She showed me a picture of him. He's a little chubby like Dink, but cute. O'course, he's not as cute as Dink."

Nadine rolled her eyes. "Oh, Lord, ain't love grand? I remember when I talked about Louie that way. I thought he was Burt Reynolds, Joe Namath and damned George Clooney, all rolled into one, and in truth, sometimes I still do. I keep seeing the boy I married when I look at him, most of the time, anyhow. He's doin' so much better since all that mess got settled and Carl Alvin got us that money. Now that Mr. Hamp has him workin' security out there at the huntin' preserve three nights a week, well, you can't believe how it's picked him up... in more ways than one," she added with a sly grin.

Wanda Faye laughed.

"I didn't remember it being that good with Louie, but, honey, here about a week ago, you'da thought Louie was one of them acrobats from Ringling Brothers. They wasn't nothin' wrong with his back that night!" Nadine said, grinning widely.

Both girls were giggling now.

"Well, Nadine, like you and Destini told me... it's my weddin'," Wanda Faye said. "Even Lollie said the same exact thing. She told me, Wanda Faye, if you want spring colors, it's your choice. It don't matter what time of year it is, by God, if you want pastels, then you have pastels."

Nadine nodded, and said, "What'd I tell you? It sounds like this gal's got a little sense."

"She does. Remember last week when I came home with my hair all done up and y'all asked if I was going to see the governor or something? Well, she's the one who done it, and she says she can't hold a candle to her Aunt Sissy."

"Well, Miss Wanda Faye, we may just have to give Miss Sissy a try at some point. Maybe before your weddin' we'll give her a call and have her do us all up. What do you say?"

"Lord, Nadine, I don't know. I ain't never been in a beauty salon in my whole life," Wanda Faye said. "I heard Mama talkin' 'bout goin' up to Miss Betty when she was younger. She said back then the ladies would get a perm and they'd put 'em under this curling machine that looked like the electric chair with all the coils and cords coming out the top of it. The ladies were told that since it might electrocute 'em, they'd have to put their feet on a rubber foot pad to keep 'em from gettin' shocked to death. That permanent solution, she said, would smell and burn their scalps. Then, Miss Betty would have to blow on their head ever' once in a while to keep the hair from catching on fire."

"Well, I sure as hell don't wanna go through that, do you?" Nadine asked her. "You reckon that's what that slogan of Miss Sissy's means? Beauty has no pain? I sure hope not!"

"No, they don't do all that now," Wanda Faye assured her. "They've come a long way in the beauty business, just like they have in nursing and medicine. It's all modern now. Lollie said Miss Sissy has the most modern, up-to-date salon in the county."

Nadine reached in her purse and pulled out a cigarette. After lighting up, she reached back in and pulled out swatches of material. In her hands were some of the most beautiful samples of dotted Swiss material in pastel colors that Wanda

Faye had ever seen. They were pale pastels like Easter eggs and interspersed with tiny daisies. Other than the pink rose, daisies were Wanda Faye's favorite flower.

"Oh, my, Lord, Nadine!" Wanda Faye gasped. "Where in the world...?"

Nadine took a drag off her cigarette and said, "Essie brought these up to Destini last night when they came to see Mama Tee. She said to have you look at them. If you like any of them, she and Destini can start working on dresses for all the little girls and for Destini and me."

"Like them? Oh, Lord, Nadine! I love the colors, the material... everything! You don't reckon people's gonna say I'm white trash or nothin' because I'm using spring colors in late fall, do you?"

"Who cares what they say? It's like Lollie told you, it's your weddin', honey."

"Yes, that's true," Wanda Faye said. "Just last week on television, Miss Margot was sayin' you got to make your own choices for special events, just like she done for that big party she gave for that famous actor, Shawn Edwards, I think his name was. She loved the color orange, so she used a lot of it for the decorations. She even had that singer Kasi Arnold sing "The Color Orange".

As the fabric samples were examined more closely and dress patterns came out of a tote bag Nadine was holding, the girls were completely engrossed in planning for the upcoming wedding.

They were in the middle of talking about the pastel colors of the helium balloons they planned to place around the fellowship hall, and getting just the right shade of crepe paper to hang from the rafters to match the pastels, when Nadine's cell phone rang.

"Head lice!" Nadine screamed. "What do you mean some of our youngun's have head lice? We'll be right there, Louie. Don't you go nowhere, and don't you make no bigger deal out of this! Yeah, I hear them youngun's cryin'. You get inside and fix them babies a glass of that Kool-Aid and give 'em some cookies, and Louie? Please keep them outside till we get there!"

Chapter 11

Racecar driver Jeff Gordon couldn't have covered the five miles from Wanda Faye's apartment out to Nadine's mobile home on the edge of town any faster than she did in Wanda Faye's old pickup.

"Head lice! Damn!" Nadine kept yelling.

"Nadine, will you please calm down?" Wanda Faye pleaded, as she held on to the dashboard for dear life. "You're gonna get us both killed! Slow down, willya? God, I knew I shouldn't have let you drive!"

Wanda Faye's words fell on deaf ears. When Nadine turned onto the dirt road leading to her house, a cloud of dust exploded behind her and then the breaks on the old truck cried like a squalling baby when she came to an abrupt stop by the white picket fence about ten yards out in front of the trailer.

Little Chet was the first one to come running over to greet them.

"Mama, please don't act mad," he said to

Wanda Faye. "Me and Victor and Jeff, we ain't got 'em, but all the girls do, and they say little Jewell's the worst. They's all crying 'cause Uncle Louie told 'em they might have to get their hair shaved off. He said that's what his mama did to his cousin one summer, who got them from some trashy people lived down there by Roaring Creek."

As Wanda Faye and Nadine continued toward the trailer, they could see the girls were upset as they ran over to them. Nadine looked over at Louie, pointed at him with her lit cigarette and simply said a firm, "Later!"

"Now, what have I done, Nadine?" Louie asked her, throwing his hands up in the air.

"Just shut the hell up, Louie! Later!" she repeated. "The first string is here now. Get your damned lunchbox and go on to work before I kill you. They ain't a jury in the county that would convict me. There's some sandwiches and cold drinks in the cooler in the back of the truck, and you can make some coffee out at Camp EZ or get Destini to do it for you. Go on, now, Louie. I appreciate you pickin' up the children, but they're all upset now, and you ain't helping matters at all."

In truth, neither Wanda Faye nor Nadine were prepared for the situation, since they'd never had lice or been exposed to anyone who had. They'd been raised in a house where the surgeon general would have done an operation any day of the week... even on the kitchen floor. One of Miss Jewell's mottos was "cleanliness is next to godliness", and even though it wasn't written in the Bible anywhere, she cleaved to it like a holy amulet. Even now, when either of the girls smelled bleach, Pine Sol or Lysol, they thought of their mama. More than just a little of her passion had been passed down to her daughters.

Louie told folks all the time that if he wanted to make Nadine or Wanda Faye happy on birthdays or Christmas, he'd get them new rubber gloves, new mops, or, if he had the money, a rebuilt vacuum cleaner. Up until they'd received the insurance settlement, Louie was always on the search for rebuilt vacuum cleaners, as well as washers and dryers. With Wanda Faye and Nadine, one could never keep pace with replacing their cleaning equipment.

They both sanitized their homes religiously at least twice a week, getting down on their knees to sponge off baseboards and taking toothbrushes to clean around bathroom fixtures.

Even though Wanda Faye had four kids and Nadine had three, you never smelled poopie diapers or the stench of urine, or anything except clean when you entered their homes. If they had to stay up until one or two in the morning washing and ironing, the children were always well dressed in clean clothes, shoes and underclothes.

Bed linens, towels, wash cloths, curtains and everything were always kept just so. Their children learned early on that their mamas meant business about keeping a tidy house, and there was never any crayon or magic marker on the walls that one often saw in homes where young children were present.

One reason for this was a warning from their mamas. The second, and most important, was the lady who stayed in Nadine and Wanda Faye's closets named Miss Switch. She didn't come out often, but when she did, she could stripe some legs and bottoms, and make a deep impression before she was put back in her living quarters.

Even though the girls had no experience with head lice, they were both adamant that their baby girls with the beautiful, long hair that was so precious to those raised in the Pentecostal faith, were not going to have their heads shaved.

Nadine turned to her sister with a look of helplessness. "What are we gonna do? Hell, I don't know what to do."

"Give me that phone," Wanda Faye said and then she punched in a phone number.

"Lollie, this is Wanda Faye. I need some help or some advice... or both."

Wanda Faye calmly explained her predicament to Lollie, who was familiar with all the children, even Nadine's kids, because Wanda Faye had shared photos with her on numerous occasions. She recalled Lollie's comment about the length of the girls' hair and how pretty they all were.

Wanda Faye considered Lollie a good friend and she had confided many things to her in the last few weeks, including the fact that if it hadn't been for Nadine, she wouldn't be in nursing school. She even told her about their lawsuit and all the money they received from it, although, in hindsight, she regretted having disclosed so much personal information.

After she finished telling her about the lice problem, Lollie insisted she bring all the kids up to her aunt's shop in Turpricone immediately.

"You bring them precious darlings on up here, Wanda Faye," Lollie told her. "You're my friend and friends help each other out. Bring them babies on up here. We'll get them straightened out."

"Oh, Lollie, thank you," Wanda Faye said.

"You tell them sweet babies to hush their crying, too, 'cause nobody's going to cut off their hair. Aunt Sissy and I know just what to do for them. She'll love y'all, and you'll love her. Nobody in that shop will know one darned thing, either. I'll tell them you're my school friends and we're going in the back room to talk. Tell all the kids to meet us at the back door."

"Thank you, again, Lollie," Wanda Faye said. "I owe you one."

"Aww, you don't owe me a thing," Lollie said. "Just come on up here."

Wanda Faye quickly rounded everyone up and told them to jump in the bed of the truck. She snatched the keys from Nadine and hopped in behind the wheel.

"Well, come on, Sis, get in!" Wanda Faye yelled to Nadine, who was standing in the middle of the yard, staring back at her.

When she finally got in the truck, she looked at Wanda Faye with tears in her eyes.

"I'm not mad at you," she told Wanda Faye. "I'm mad at Louie and the way he handled things. It's bad enough the kids got lice, but to scare 'em all like that? That was just wrong."

"Aw, don't be too mad at him," Wanda Faye said. "At least he picked up the kids. He coulda' just left 'em there at school and made you go get 'em."

"Yeah, I guess you're right," Nadine said, and then she heaved a big, long sigh and settled back in her seat.

"You kids sit down back there!" Wanda Faye yelled out the window. "I don't wanna lose any of ya!" she added and then she started up the dirt road toward the highway.

"Maybe the wind'll blow all them nits outta their hair," Nadine mumbled, once they were cruising down the road.

Wanda Faye looked over at her and the next

thing she knew she was laughing so hard she could barely see to drive. Nadine joined in and it seemed the laughter they shared together had a soothing effect on both of them.

Meanwhile, neither one of them had a clue what Lollie was really up to, but they'd soon find out.

Chapter 12

When Wanda Faye arrived at Miss Sissy's shop in Turpricone, she parked in the back of the building and told all the kids to wait right where they were until she came back out for them. Then, she and Nadine walked around to the front door and went inside.

The first thing Wanda Faye noticed was the music that was echoing throughout the salon. Elvis Presley was singing a classic song from his gospel CD called, "He Touched Me". Just hearing his voice gave her a chill up and down her spine. She loved listening to him sing, especially gospel songs.

Lollie spotted the girls right away and quickly ushered them into the back room.

"I'll be right back, ladies," she told them. "Aunt Sissy will be out in just a few minutes, too, so just have a seat over there."

Lollie pointed to a couple of comfortable looking upholstered chairs near where the sinks were lined up against one wall. Nadine, who seemed nervous as a goat, went over to the window in the back of the room, evidently so she could keep a watchful eye on the children.

As Wanda Faye sat and waited, she could hear a female voice coming from inside a room straight across from her. The door was cracked open enough for her to see a woman, whom she assumed to be Miss Sissy, sitting in front of an antique wooden desk. She had her back to her with the telephone receiver to her ear, and she was acting all giddy like a child who just saw Santa Claus for the first time.

"Wow, she really does look young," Wanda Faye thought, when she got a glimpse of her profile.

Miss Sissy was thumbing through what looked to be a Neiman Marcus catalogue. Wanda Faye had just browsed through one the other day at the Vo-Tech and was shocked at how expensive everything was in the mail order store.

"Amber? Is that your name?" she heard Miss Sissy ask. "Well, this is Eileen Paquette. Oh, you recognize my voice, you sweet thing. I just love you Dallas folks. You can call me Miss Sissy, honey. All my friends do. Maybe one day I'll meet you in person and we can be the best of friends."

There was a pause, as if the person on the other end was talking, and then Miss Sissy spoke again.

"Yes, baby, do you have your holiday catalogue there handy? I want to order the St. John's evening suit. Yes, honey, the white one with the gold trim. Yes, isn't it pretty? I want to put it on my Neiman's charge. It's one-thousand dollars, right?"

Wanda Faye's jaw nearly dropped to the floor.

"A thousand dollars for one evening suit?" she thought, clearly stunned that someone would pay so much for just one outfit.

After a bit more conversation, Miss Sissy hung up the phone. When she walked out of the office, she was humming an old hymn, "Bring Them In".

Just then, Lollie appeared and she told Wanda Faye to bring the kids in through the backdoor. When they all came inside, Miss Sissy greeted them with a huge smile and even spoke to the little girls as if she was one of them.

"Such beautiful girls," she said. "Beautiful little girls and beautiful big girls," she added, as she placed her arms around Wanda Faye and Nadine.

Iris Wesson, the wife of the local Circuit Judge had just stepped into the room, expecting to get her hair washed. Miss Sissy spotted her out of the corner of her eye.

"I just love pretty girls, don't you, Miss Iris? Go sit over there in that chair a minute," Miss Sissy practically ordered her. "Mark! Mark, honey! Come refill Miss Iris' coffee cup... two teaspoons of sugar, okay? How about another slice of that pound cake, Miss Iris? You can stand it. You got the figure of a twenty-year-old."

Iris seemed to be quite perturbed by the fact Miss Sissy was putting her on hold. Wanda Faye swore she could hear her mumbling about a shouting-church, happy-clappy bunch and their little tangle-haired children.

Iris finally smiled. It was a tight-lipped smile, though, and then she nodded at Miss Sissy. Seconds later, she was ushered out of the room by Mark, Miss Sissy's shop assistant, who had her coffee and pound cake on a silver tray.

Wanda Faye recognized Mark from school. He was in the same class as Lollie. She thought it was quite amusing as she watched him sashay out of the room, swishing his behind like a sixteen-year-old girl. It was hard to tell how many shades of blonde he had in his hair because it was spiked up and sticking out every which way. He was almost waif-like in appearance, she thought.

Seconds later, she heard him call out to Lollie, asking if she wanted him to start the pedicure on Miss Iris. He even said he'd get the pedi-soap ready.

"Pedi-soap?" Wanda Faye thought, shaking her head. "Good grief."

"No, you won't!" Miss Sissy piped up. "You come on back here, Mark! I need you back here!"

When Mark returned, Wanda Faye knew his worst fears were realized. Miss Sissy pointed him toward the sink where several bottles of lice shampoo were waiting for him. It was then that Miss Sissy closed the door between the front salon and the back rooms.

"Mark, put that smock on and them gloves and come here," she said, as she hastened over to the sinks. "We're going to shampoo these angels. Then, I want you to get that little comb, 'cause you're gonna pick as many of these nits from their hair as you can possibly see."

Mark did a little whole-body shiver as he listened to his boss crank out orders.

"Lollie, you get up on that little stepladder and screw these in," Miss Sissy continued, and she handed her a package of 150-watt light bulbs. "They've got more voltage, and Mark, here's my magnifying light, the big one. When you finish with the treatment, and you've seen all the nits you can see with the naked eye, you shampoo again. Then, you put these children under this magnifying light. Lollie, you go to that other sink and do the same thing," she ordered her faithful servants. "This is gonna take a while."

Miss Sissy looked over at Wanda Faye and Nadine and gave them both a curt smile.

"When these angels leave here, they'll be nit-free or my name ain't Miss Sissy Paquette," she told them. "Now, when y'all get home, you're gonna have to get scalding water and go over every inch of your house with it... and use bleach.

Then, you'll need to wipe down all your beds, the furniture... everything in the house with scalding water and bleach... or Lysol, if you got it."

Wanda Faye and Nadine looked at one another, as if they had just been doomed to hell by the almighty Miss Sissy.

"You'll have to strip all the beds, and then wash all the bed clothes and all the children's clothes. Keep using the shampoo for the amount of time it tells you on the box. It's high-priced, but it does the trick."

"We'll do it, Miss Sissy," Nadine assured her.

"Then, I want you to go to that school and insist that a head check be done in their classrooms," Miss Sissy kept on. "Now, here's another thing, and I don't usually do this, but y'all have had a bad day, both of you," she said. "You just leave these angels to Mark and Lollie, and later on I'll give both y'all a Roux White Minx rinse. Y'all got beautiful hair, but it's a little damaged from the sun. You'll both feel better and look better when I'm done. Now, the lice treatment ain't on the house, but the rinse for y'all is... this time. You are both sweet things."

With that, she gave Wanda Faye and Nadine a big hug.

"Don't feel bad about this," Miss Sissy consoled them. "Hell, it even happened to the sheriff's kids last year. These lice is ever'where. The only place you won't find 'em is in black people's hair. You see, their hair shafts are shaped different than white folks and lice won't hold on it. Just know that your children won't get lice from Destini's little girl. What's that child's name?"

"Easter Bunnye," Wanda Faye said.

"How's that?" Miss Sissy asked, scrunching up her face.

"Easter Bunnye," Wanda Faye repeated. "Destini's daughter's name is Easter Bunnye, but we all call her Bunnye."

"Oh, yes, that's it. I forgot. I love it. She's such a sweet, little thing. She looks like a little chocolate cherub. I see her up here once in a while when Destini comes and picks up hair care items for the folks staying out at Camp EZ. Even before Lollie told me about you girls, I'd heard about what good girls y'all was from Destini."

Miss Sissy then excused herself, saying she had some customers to attend to and would be back later.

Having never been in a beauty shop before, Wanda Faye was in complete awe. All of a sudden, here she was in the best salon in the county, being treated so sweetly by the one and only beautician to the county's elected officials and all the upper crust. It was almost too much to fathom at the moment.

As Wanda Faye looked around, she felt as if she was living in a fantasy world. The salon was done in white and gold, and all the styling chairs and shampoo chairs were done in antique gold upholstery. All the sinks and counter tops, as well as the ceramic tiled floors were gleaming in whiteness. Even the dryer chairs were upholstered in antique gold, and the windows of the shop were decorated with valances in antique gold and white.

Between the reception area and the back room where the sinks and hair dryers were located was a four foot section of lattice work that she noticed when she first came in. Miss Sissy had tastefully intertwined silk ivy, magnolia greenery, and white magnolia blossoms all through the intricate woodwork.

Wanda Faye recalled one of Miss Margot's recent television shows about the London Hotel. Margot said she was going to coin an old phrase used by the late Diana Vreeland, a high class women's fashion icon and magazine editor. She said Miss Vreeland would have said the London Hotel was "luxury in depth."

Looking around her now, Wanda Faye felt that description fit Miss Sissy's shop perfectly.

Just as Miss Sissy said earlier, the entire process was taking a long time. With all the shampooing and nit picking going on, more than two hours had passed already. At one point, Miss Sissy sent Lollie across the street to the dollar store to get each of the little girls a large soft drink, as well as coloring books and individual boxes of crayons to keep them occupied in between treatments.

Wanda Faye and Nadine gently reminded the girls a few times to thank Miss Sissy and Lollie for all they were doing, and they did so perfunctorily.

"What sweet manners," Miss Sissy said, smiling. "It shows they've had some good raising. I can tell you, in today's world, most children haven't had one dab of proper raising. Praise the Lord for these sweet angels."

As Mark was attending to blow drying each of the girls' hair, Miss Sissy and Lollie started applying the Roux White Minx rinse to Wanda Faye's and Nadine's hair.

"Use more de-tangler," Miss Sissy told Lollie, who was working on Nadine.

Miss Sissy seemed to be in her element, constantly gabbing as she worked on Wanda Faye's hair.

"I declare," she said. "These beautiful heads of hair remind me of my own when I was growing up in Beaumont, Mississippi. Daddy was the gin manager there for a Mr. Carson, who owned a huge place called Rawhide Plantation. Back then, Mama would do my hair in long braids, and when I got a little older, she'd pull it back in a ponytail for me. My hair was about the color of yours, Nadine."

"You mean dishwater blonde?" Nadine asked

with a chuckle.

"I prefer to call it golden sunshine," Miss Sissy said. "That's what it reminds me of, pure golden sunshine. Mama was a holy roller from head to foot, yes ma'am. She could pick that big, white guitar Daddy bought for her in Memphis, and Lord, that woman could sing. I can still hear her."

Miss Sissy suddenly broke into a sweet rendition of an old gospel song called, "The Eastern Gate".

"I will meet you in the morning, just inside the Eastern gate, then be ready faithful pilgrim, do not tarry nor be late..."

By the time she finished singing, Wanda Faye noticed she was crying. Her thick, black mascara was running down her cheeks, leaving dark streaks behind.

"I'm sorry, girls," she said, sniffling. "Meeting the two of you and these precious babies, and seeing this beautiful hair took me on a trip down memory lane. I declare, I'm getting old and silly."

"No, ma'am," Nadine said. "I don't think you're silly at all, Miss Sissy. I think the love of Jesus lives in you, and you show it to people who need it. Your sign out front may say beautician, but I believe you are one of God's special angels, a missionary sent here to this county from the state of Mississippi to spread His word through your voice, your beauty, and your talent as a hairdresser."

"Aw, thank you, Nadine," Miss Sissy said, as she took a tissue to her eyes.

"When I heard you singing, I coulda' swore it was Sophie Martin," Nadine went on. "You look kinda like her, too. I mean that as a compliment Miss Sissy. Sophie Martin is one of my all time favorites."

"Oh, my beautiful sunshine girls," Miss Sissy said. "I declare, I don't know when I've felt better about myself. Y'all are the missionaries, not me. I'm the one who's received the blessing today."

Chapter 13

Sticker shock was about to hit Wanda Faye and Nadine full on as they prepared to leave the salon. Before they went out front to settle their bill, Wanda Faye rounded up all the kids and ushered them out the backdoor and into the bed of the pickup.

"I got my eye on y'all, so behave," she warned them.

She nearly head-butted Mark when she came barreling back inside. He looked completely exhausted, but relieved at the same time, as he carefully carried a bowl of what she assumed was the pedi-soap solution for Iris Wesson's feet. She watched him sashay off again and had to stifle a laugh.

"Well, Miss Sissy, you've been so sweet and good to us," Wanda Faye said. "How can we ever thank you?"

"You can thank me by keeping your gorgeous locks in beautiful condition," she said. "Remember my motto, beauty has no pain."

"Miss Sissy, our hair won't ever look this good again," Wanda Faye said, as she admired herself one last time in the mirror.

"Oh, yes, it can, and it will," Miss Sissy told her, as they walked out front to the cash register. "I have some products I can sell you girls that will make you both look this good, if not better, every day."

By the time Miss Sissy finished whispering to the girls about what to do as a follow-up for the lice and nit treatment, and showing them hair care products and explaining how to use them, Nadine had dropped in the neighborhood of three-hundred-and-fifty dollars.

The lice treatments cost a whopping one-hundred dollars, and then Nadine evidently felt obligated to purchase another two-hundred-and-fifty dollars worth of shampoo, conditioner, Roux White Minx Rinse, de-tangler, hair spray, and a couple of brushes for both her and Wanda Faye. After that, she made appointments for the two of them for the following week to have their hair trimmed and some highlights added.

Miss Sissy had told them they really needed to "bring the sunshine out" in their hair before the homecoming at the House of Prayer, which was coming up in a few weeks. She made additional appointments for an all-day beauty treatment for the two of them the day before the homecoming.

"Should we make an appointment for Mama, too?" Nadine asked Wanda Faye.

"Are you kidding? Mama would never come. She'll be too busy at the church with Brother Linton and Sister Velma and Sister Mary Lee getting everything just so for homecoming."

"Is there anything we can do for Destini?" Nadine asked Miss Sissy.

"Now, girls, I know Destini's a good friend of yours, but I don't usually do the hair of the colored," she said. "I do know a girl from over in Tallahassee, though, who comes here to visit her mama two Saturdays each month. She's the best on black folks' hair I've ever seen. She's got a little place around there off Carver Drive by her mama's house."

"Oh, yeah, I've been by there hundreds of times," Nadine said.

"I'll call her and get Destini in with her the day y'all have the homecoming, but I'm here to tell you, she ain't cheap. Get your pocketbooks ready. All them chemicals they use on colored folks' hair is as high as giraffe titties," she added, and then she paused for a moment. "Ohh, goodness, y'all, excuse me," she said, blushing.

Everyone in the shop had heard her little faux pas and they were all laughing, even Iris Wesson, although, it seemed to hurt her to laugh, Wanda Faye thought.

"What about the little angels?" Lollie interjected, once the laughter subsided. "Don't we want to do their hair, too? You know, for the wedding? How many are there?"

"Well, we got seven all together," Nadine said. "Four girls and three boys."

"Perfect," Miss Sissy said. "Oh, this is wonderful. Lollie, just mark my appointment book off for that whole afternoon. We'll do the boys first and then your husband, Nadine. Or, we can do your fiancé first, Wanda Faye, and then we can start on the little girls before we do you two. Do you think your two men might need a haircut?"

"We'll ask them," Nadine said. "We'll let you know tomorrow."

"You do that, hon," Miss Sissy said. "Do that for Miss Sissy. Oh, and Wanda Faye, darling, I forgot to tell you what a pretty ring you have. Who's the lucky man, sugar?"

"His name is Drayfuss Lowell, but everybody calls him Dink," Wanda Faye said, smiling. "He's the sweetest, kindest man in the world."

Wanda Faye wasn't sure, but for a moment she thought Miss Sissy was going to faint. Her face turned white as the tiled floor, and beads of perspiration began pooling around her hairline and across the bridge of her nose.

"Are you all right, Miss Sissy?" she asked her. "You ain't sick, are you?"

"No, just a little flushed, dear," she said. "I'll just sit down here for a minute. Lollie, will you tell Mark to bring me a short Coke and that pack of BC Powders? There's nothing as good for a bad, old headache as a BC with a Coke," she twittered on, seeming to Wanda Faye as if something was really wrong with her.

"Are you sure you're okay?" Wanda Faye asked her again.

"Oh, yes, I'm fine," Miss Sissy said. "I guess it's just my time of life. You girls will get there if you live long enough, and I know you will."

Wanda Faye was about to tell her she didn't look old enough to be bothered with menopause already, but Mark showed up with her meds and Miss Sissy just kept on talking.

"Mark, bring a couple of my signature bags for these angels to put their products in. You know, honey, the special ones. I want each of them to have one," Miss Sissy said.

"Two of your special bags, Miss Sissy?" he asked. "Are you sure?"

"Yes, I'm sure, Mark," she said, beginning to sound agitated.

Seconds later, Mark emerged from the back room with two canvas tote bags that were done in a gold lame finish. On the side was embossed a photo of Miss Sissy with her motto written underneath in cursive, *"Beauty has no pain."*

"Oh, these are beautiful," Wanda Faye said. "Thank you so much."

"Yes, they are beautiful, aren't they? And so

are you," Miss Sissy said. "It's been a blessing seeing you girls, and I'll be seeing you again soon, real soon."

Chapter 14

Miss Sissy's confession

Miss Sissy had just finished combing out Iris Wesson's hair, her last appointment of the day. As soon as Iris paid her bill and walked out of the shop, Miss Sissy turned out the lights, locked the door, and pulled down the window shade. Lollie had already gone home for the day and Mark was finishing up the sweeping and mopping.

"Are you feeling better, Miss Sissy?" Mark asked her.

"Not really, darling," she said. "Oh, Mark, what am I going to do? What if she finds out?"

"Unless you start your blabbering and tell her yourself, I really don't think she'll be any the wiser. After all, it's only you and me who know what happened."

"He was a pretty thing, wasn't he? When I first came into town and he worked on my car, oh, goodness, I just fell in love with him."

"So did I," Mark said. "Too bad he didn't swing my way, though. Me and Dink could have had a lot of fun together."

"It was a short affair, but Mark, I do believe it was the most intense relationship I've ever had with a man. I felt like I had died and gone to heaven."

"Yes, it's a shame you gave him up," Mark said, as he sat down beside her in one of the shampoo chairs.

"Well, when you land one of the county's biggest fish as your man, you pretty much have no choice."

"I know, honey, I know," Mark said. "I'm sure you enjoy driving that big ol' Cadillac a lot more than that old Ford you were driving when you were seeing Dink."

"Beauty has no pain, Mark," she said. "But it sure as hell was painful giving up that beautiful Dink."

"I'm sure it was. I'm also sure that's why you gave those girls those expensive tote bags. Let's just hope they never find out the truth."

"Yes, Mark," she said with a sigh. "It would be so devastating for Wanda Faye, not to mention the hell I'd catch from Dink for letting the cat out of the bag, so to speak."

Miss Sissy went over to the CD player and popped in her favorite golden country oldie by the Kendall's, fast forwarding it to the song she and Dink had loved so much, “Heaven’s Just a Sin Away”.

As she sang along with the lyrics, Mark joined her in the chorus, and then the two of them waltzed around the floor together, keeping perfect time with the melody.

“Don’t worry, Miss Sissy, everything is going to be just fine,” Mark consoled her, as she shed a few tears.

“I know it will, honey. Dink is just a part of my past now. I’ll just have to be a little more careful not to let on about any of this to Wanda Faye.”

“Yes, dear, just think happy thoughts,” Mark said. “Think about that new St. John’s suit you’ll be wearing out with your gentleman friend when you go to Jim Campbell’s open house at Christmastime.”

“Yes, you’re absolutely right,” she said, and her face brightened, as she admired the diamond tennis bracelet, the stunning golden charm bracelet, and the big pearl and diamond ring she was wearing on her left hand. “I feel very blessed.”

Chapter 15

Over the next few weeks, there was a whirlwind of activity for Wanda Faye, Nadine and Destini, as they busied themselves with their respective jobs and pursuits, aside from all the wedding planning.

Wanda Faye was blissfully happy going to school, spending quality time with Dink, helping Destini at Camp EZ, and spending as much time as she could with her children.

Nadine passed her days volunteering at the local elementary school, getting all the kids ready for school, picking them up in the afternoon, getting Louie ready for work at Camp EZ three or four nights a week, and making sure she had enough honey-do's to keep him busy every day.

Destini was overjoyed that Bunnye was in pre-kindergarten now, having the time of her life as part of the Wanda Faye/Nadine/Destini children's group.

Bunnye also accompanied the other children to the House of Prayer and was part of the Bible

Drill team, right alongside the others. She had been going there so long that the highly rural, provincial, all-white congregation looked upon her as just another one of the children. She was as likely as not to wind up in Brother Linton's lap up at the pulpit before the services began.

Wanda Faye and Dink had their pre-marital counseling session with Brother Linton in mid-October, and he gave them each a book about marriage and responsibility. He also talked with them and prayed with them. He told them how honored he was to be chosen to join them in holy matrimony later in the fall. Wanda Faye assured him they wouldn't have chosen anyone else to do the honors.

On the day he counseled with them, Wanda Faye thought he seemed more preoccupied than usual. When she questioned him about it, he told her and Dink that Jerri Faye hadn't been doing well lately.

"Oh, she's still happy as a lark, but she's lost her appetite for most anything to eat," he said. "She gets tired much more easily than she used to, although, you'd never know it when she sees you and Nadine. You girls will never know what you mean to her. She worships you. She's always talking about how pretty you are and that you're her sisters."

Without wasting any more time, Brother Linton suggested they get on with the counseling. At the end of their session, Wanda Faye felt confident about her decision to marry Dink. They both seemed to be on the same page about everything that was discussed.

As they were preparing to leave, Wanda Faye turned to the preacher to ask one last question.

"Brother Linton, I ain't a deacon or a preacher, but before me and Dink leave, do you mind if I say a little prayer?"

Brother Linton seemed taken by surprise at her request, and for good reason. All her life, Wanda Faye had been the quieter, more reticent sister. Even though she was older than Nadine, she always let her sister lead in most instances.

"Why, no, child, I'd be happy for you to pray," Brother Linton said.

Wanda Faye's heart was heavily burdened as she closed her eyes. A bad feeling had come over her. It was a feeling of heartache and pain. In this instance, it was about Jerri Faye's sickness, as well as the pain she knew both Brother Linton and Sister Velma were experiencing.

There was something more, though. Something she couldn't quite put her finger on. It was almost as if life, right now, was just too darned happy. Throughout her life, she had learned not to trust happiness as a full time occupant of one's heart. Happiness was only a visitor who came to see you from time to time. Sometimes it stayed longer than others, but it always went home.

Her heart felt the same way it did when she had to say goodbye to Nadine the one time Chester grudgingly allowed her to come visit when she was living up in Ludowici.

Wanda Faye asked Dink and Brother Linton to hold hands with her as they kneeled on the floor.

"Lord," she began. "This here's Wanda Faye. I know I ain't been much in praying out loud, but I'm wanting to say thank you. Thank you first for saving my soul. I ain't been that good of a servant, but you have never failed me. Thank you for my precious babies, Lord, and for sending me a good man in Dink. I love him, Lord, and I aim to make him a good wife."

She felt Dink's hand squeeze hers even tighter as she continued.

"Thank you, Lord, for my family, my church family, and all my friends. I praise you, Lord, for letting me go to nursing school. Thank you for Brother Linton and Sister Velma, for their testimony and love, and for what they've meant to this little church."

Wanda Faye paused for a moment and took a deep breath.

"Now, Lord, I'm begging you, please bless sweet Jerri Faye. She's your special angel, Jesus, and we know how special she is. Heal her, Lord, if it be your will, and help us to serve you with the same joy and gladness that she has given us all these years. One more thing, Jesus, before I finish up, bless Destini, Mama Tee and Bunnye. I love them, Lord, and they ain't never been no better folks in the world, white or black, dear Jesus."

Since Wanda Faye felt like she now had a captive audience, she didn't want to leave anyone out, so she continued.

"Bless our president, and all of them in the military, all the sick folks, and those who have lost loved ones, and, Jesus, bless Miss Sissy, Lollie, and especially, Lord, I pray you will continue to bless Miss Margot Smith. She's meant so much to me, Jesus, as she has to so many. I thank you for all my blessings, and, Lord, help me and Dink to be a good example to our children and in this community. Again, thank you, Jesus, for being so good to me and blessing me. I'm getting ready to say goodbye for now, Jesus, but I just want you to know that I really love you, and I praise your name, Lord, for being so good to me, even when I didn't deserve it. In your precious name I pray, Amen."

By the time she finished, Brother Linton and Dink were both weeping, so much so, that they had to turn their faces away from her for a few moments to wipe away the tears they had shed.

As they arose from the floor, Wanda Faye thought about the day Miss Margot asked her audience, "Do you know what it feels like to be truly encouraged and lifted?"

At the core of Wanda Faye's heart was still a burden; a deep, gnawing feeling that all was not well, but as she got up from her knees, she felt more encouraged than she had in a long time.

Her fears, however, were realized the next afternoon when she stopped by her mailbox. There, on top of the advertising circulars and a couple of utility bills, was a letter. She could see it was Chester's handwriting on the envelope.

"This can't be good news," she thought.

In more than just a fleeting manner, she recalled the feeling she had yesterday before she prayed. When she went back inside, she sat down at the kitchen table and opened the letter, noting again the familiar handwriting.

"Dear Wanda Faye,

My time up here in prison is growing short. I get out of jail two weeks from today. I want you to know that even though we are divorced, I want to see my children when I'm out of here. I know I told you I never wanted to see them again, but I plan on coming down to Florida as soon as I'm free and spending the day with them babies.

There's another thing I want to tell you, but I won't put it in this letter. Something about your mama and my visits with her while we were married. Even though you and me is split up,

Miss Jewell has prayed for me all along. She even contacted a preacher she knew up here in Georgia to come out to the jail and visit me from time to time.

I am not threatening you, Wanda Faye, I'm just telling you. I plan on seeing the children. I hear you are seeing your old flame, Dink. He better not put a hand on one of my children or I'll be back in this jail, and the next time it will be for murder.

Your ex, but still loving husband in the eyes of God, Chester.

Over and over, his words whirled through her mind. She read and re-read the letter several more times. By the time the children came home, she wasn't in her usual chair watching Margot Smith on the television. She was lying on her bed in a darkened room.

When Nadine and Destini came to pick up their kids and saw all of the children in the living room watching a cartoon video, they both looked at one another.

"Uh-oh, something's up," Destini said. "I can feel it in my bones."

"You kids go on outside and play," Nadine ordered them. "Go on, scoot."

Once all the kids dispersed out the front door, Nadine and Destini went into the bedroom. There was Wanda Faye lying face down on the bed. Nadine sat down next to her and Destini sat down on a chair beside the nightstand.

"Well," Destini said. "Don't see no belts or cords hanging from the rafter with no nooses made up, and no razors or pills beside the bed. What I do see is crumpled up tissues strewed all over the place, so we can rule out you being pregnant or you woulda' killed yourself already. Come clean, girl. You and Dink got trouble?"

Wanda Faye turned over and sat up, looking like death warmed over. Then, she reached under her pillow, pulled out the letter and handed it to Destini, who read it out loud.

As she read it, Wanda Faye started crying again, so Nadine comforted her by rubbing her back. Before the pity party could spin into over-drive, Destini took the lead.

"Shut that mess up, now. Wanda Faye," she scolded her. "Cryin' ain't gonna change a damn thing here. Hell, don't be cryin'. The only thing cryin' does is make you pee less."

"What?" Nadine asked, shocked, but amused at her statement.

"Hits the damned truff, Mama Tee always says. The more you cry, the less you piss. So, Wanda Faye, baby, you may not pee for the next two, maybe three days, and to think you've let some no good bastard like Chester put you in this state."

"Well, it took me by surprise," Wanda Faye

said, still sniffling back tears. “I wasn’t expecting this.”

“Well, you lived with him long enough,” Destini said. “You damn sure expected something. You know he ain’t no sweetheart. Anybody who would beat you with belts till you had marks on you, and then want to get on top of you… sick bastard. You knew he was gonna do something. You just didn’t know what or when. At least, this way, the crazy son of a bitch gave us a little warning, and the rest we’ll find out later.”

“How you gonna do that?” Nadine asked.

“Honey chile,” Destini started, putting on her best Mammy imitation from *Gone with the Wind*. “Don’t y’all worry y’all’s pretty little heads ‘bout this problem. No, ma’am. I’ll take care of this. Y’all go on like nothin’s happened, or at least try to act that way. Don’t let on to the children, and don’t let on to Miss Jewell.”

Destini had the girls’ full attention now.

“Wanda Faye,” she said. “Every morning, I’m gonna come into town and check your mailbox. If Sugar Daddy sends any more letters, I’ll be the one to read ‘em. You don’t need to know nothin’ ‘bout them. If I don’t miss my guess, after this first one, they’ll be others, and each one, when you don’t acknowledge it, will tell me more and more. Yes, ma’am, Mama Tee always say with a little money and a little time you can find out ‘bout whatever you want, and, honey, I got both.

A little money and a little time. Yes, indeedy do."

"Oh, Destini, don't be doin' nothin' crazy, now," Wanda Faye told her.

"Hey, this kinda business is my kind of business. I always loved readin' them Nancy Drew mysteries, but if Nancy had been black, she'd been a whole lot louder, and them that did wrong woulda suffered a whole lot more. This bastard's gonna suffer, baby, just as God sits on high and looks down low. This letter writin' thing is gonna stop, and the one place he'll never wanna come for a vacation or a visit will be the state of Florida. Just hearin' someone hum "Suwannee River" will cause him to shit on hisself."

"Destini!" Nadine gasped. "How in the hell...?"

"Well, you know, honey, most white folks think we all look alike, and in Mr. bass guitar playing, wife beater's ass case, he ain't never laid eyes on me," Destini said. "Never has. Oh, I know, Wanda Faye, he heard about me, but he ain't never seen me. That helps. Helps a whole lot. Just another nigger in his book. Well, this nigger is sho' nuff goin' be a nigger. One he's heard about and been scared of all his life. Yes, indeed, Nancy Drew Darkey goin' get her little mystery spy glass and off we go."

Wanda Faye was beside herself and was clearly shocked at Destini's proclamations.

"The two of you, get on that horn and order

the flowers for the church homecoming," Destini kept on. "You know how yo' mama loves fall colors. I got the passports for her and Sister Velma here in my pocketbook. Nadine, you got the travel folders with the plane tickets, itinerary and everything. She'll have two weeks from next Sunday till they leave on that trip, and when she comes back, Miss Wanda Faye, you and Dink will have about four weeks till y'alls weddin'. Lots to do in just a short time. Amidst all the plannin' and goin's on, Nancy Drew Darkey here goin' be easing around doing her job. Yes, ma'am. All kinds of goin's on."

A few minutes later, the three girls were in the living room of Wanda Faye's small apartment enjoying a much-needed cup of coffee. Through the front screened door, they could hear the children laughing and playing outside.

Margot Smith was on the television sporting a light beige sweater with a pair of camel-colored slacks, while a beautiful pair of pearl earrings framed her face. Her show was just about to end.

"We all have mountaintop experiences, but it is in the valley that the grass is usually the greenest, if we take time to look," Margot said to her audience. "It is out of those valley experiences that, at times, we can become our most creative and imaginative."

Destini held up her coffee cup and turned to the girls.

"Nadine... Wanda Faye, my two best friends in the whole world, I have a rhyming toast I'd like to share," Destini began. "Let's drink to the mountain and the valley so low. Let's drink to the fast and let's drink to the slow. Let's drink to our friendship, it's one that will last, and let's drink that the past will stay in the past."

All the girls raised their coffee cups and lightly clinked them together before taking a sip. Wanda Faye could tell that the bad feeling she'd had the day she prayed with Brother Linton was beginning to ease up some now. Part of the burden was still there, but it was lighter than just a short while ago.

Chapter 16

Chester Easley's prison

Chester Easley discovered early on that prison life in Georgia's State Penitentiary was much harder than he thought it was going to be. He had always considered himself, as did others in and around Ludowici, as a manly man. Nothing, however, could have prepared him for what resided inside the walls of this hell on earth.

The day of his arrival was one he knew he would never forget. After the initial processing, which was demeaning enough, in and of itself, it was time to check into his new hotel room where he would be spending the next three years.

Along the way to his cell – and it was a long walk, especially with the shackles around his ankles – he kept hearing a high-pitched chanting that sounded like something between a scream and a whoop. In fact, the more he kept hearing it, the more certain he was that it was a whoop, whoop, whoop sound. It grew steadily louder, with an accompanying whirring noise, as if something was shooting through the air within the prison.

Goose bumps the size of PeeWee marbles popped out all over his body, as his body flushed hot, and then turned nearly as cold as ice. His stomach felt like it was in knots, and there was a steady stream of hot liquid coming up from his stomach to his lips.

He was beyond nauseous, as the whooping sounds continued. They were more frightening and primal than anything he had ever heard in his life, even out in the woods around Ludowici.

Once, he heard two panthers fighting deep in the swamp. It had been close to dark and he never forgot the sound. It was something almost other-worldly. This steady whirring sound and the continuous whooping he was hearing now was more like a giant, carnivorous bird that was preparing to pounce on its prey, like the ones in those old dinosaur films.

"What *is* that?" he asked the guard who was escorting him to his cell.

"Oh, boy, don't you know? They're greeting you," the guard told him.

Chester just stared at him for a second, not quite understanding what he meant. According to the tag on his shirt, the guard's name was Deputy Fleming.

"You're the new boy on the block," Deputy

Fleming said, with an almost wicked smile on his face. "They're giving you their little greeting call. You hear that whirring noise? It's a lock or a piece of steel one of 'em's got in a sock or a stocking. Maybe a couple of 'em. Sooner or later, you goin' get your inaugural marks, just like everybody else who comes to this cell. Yes, sir, they sure are glad to see you, inmate Easley."

"You mean you know about this, and you don't try to do anything about it?" Chester asked him.

Deputy Fleming laughed a big belly laugh and then spit out a wad of chewing tobacco over his shoulder.

"Inmate Easley," he said, clearing his throat. "I got six more months till my retirement. At that time, me and the ol' lady's gonna enjoy ourselves down in Putnam County, Florida, on the St. John's River. I got a big lot there by the river and we're gonna fish, fish, fish, and just kick back and enjoy. I been waiting for this for thirty-three long years, boy. Most of them years dealing with nothings, pieces of trash and human shit, just like you. If you think I'm gonna worry my ass off about some of these sorry niggers, spics, or pieces of white trash who are in here beatin' the shit out of you, think again. I don't give a shit. If they kill you, I don't give a shit."

Chester suddenly wished he was already dead.

"So, friend," Deputy Fleming continued. "You better be looking after yourself and watch your step, 'cause when the doors lock and the lights go out, it can get mighty lonesome. Nice looking, young thing like you... if you play your cards right, you won't have to take many ass beatin's. 'Course, you may have to do something else with that behind o'yours, but if you decide to be generous with it to the right one around here, they won't be whippin' you. But, that's up to you, boy. Like I told you, I don't give a shit what happens to you."

"I ain't no queer," Chester said, knowing full well to what the guard was referring.

"Oh, son, all of us is a little queer. We may not admit it, but we're all just a little queer. Everybody's got a little something that somebody else wants. Sometimes if a person is able to give up a little something, he might gain a whole lot more. It just all depends."

"Depends on what?" Chester asked, still wishing he was dead.

"You might find that giving up a little something will be easier than you think. Them whoops and them hard metal objects in them socks and stockings can hit mighty hard on you. Look over there."

Deputy Fleming pointed to a young man, probably eighteen years of age, sweeping what looked to be a recreation room. His entire forehead, from his scalp down to the top of his lips, was bluish-black, and when he smiled at the guard, Chester noticed most of his front teeth were knocked out. One of his eyes was swollen almost shut, and the other one was so bloodshot you couldn't tell there was an eyeball in the socket. His lips were cut, and his upper arms were black and blue all over. His forearms were almost completely bandaged up.

"What happened to him?" Chester asked.

"Oh, he got the welcome wagon about the third day he was here," Deputy Fleming said. "Poor thing had one of the prettiest sets of white teeth you ever seen. Bad looking now, though, and I wonder, even with surgery, if that nose and them eyes is ever gonna be completely healed."

"Damn," Chester muttered.

"Things could've been different for him, had he just been willing to give away just a little something," Deputy Fleming kept on. "Now, since he's wound up giving it away, anyway, his pretty boy looks are gone. You'll learn soon enough, boy."

When the two of them finally arrived at the cell, Deputy Fleming unlocked the door, and then took off Chester's ankle shackles. Standing right in front of them, just a few feet away, was the biggest mountain of a man Chester had ever seen in his life. He was the color of coffee with heavy cream, and had four gold teeth in the front.

When Chester mustered up the nerve to look him dead straight in the face, he saw he had eyes about the color of slate and the longest eyelashes he'd ever seen on a man. His eyes had a gleam to them and it wasn't a happy gleam. It was more like a snake that had its sights on you right before striking with its deadly venom.

The big elephant of a man he'd be sharing a cell with had huge, muscular arms, and on his right forearm was branded the letter "D". It was a huge brand that had been healed over for a long time, as far as he could tell.

"This is your new home away from home, inmate Easley," Deputy Fleming said. "Meet your cell mate, inmate Dexter. I'm sure y'all goin' get along real fine... real fine."

Deputy Fleming took off Chester's handcuffs and then turned on his heels, locking the cell door behind him. At the sound of the clanging metal, Chester's heart felt as if it had dropped to the basement. Then the lights went out. The only illumination on the cell block was a dim red light coming from the exit sign about six cells down.

Not really knowing what to do next or what to expect, Chester figured he'd sit down on his bunk and try to get some shuteye. Before he could do so, however, inmate Dexter came up behind him.

"You got a first name, boy? Don't like using these last names," he said.

Chester was so spooked he was afraid to turn

around, so he spoke over his shoulder.

"Name's Chester... Chester Easley."

"They call's me Big D or Daddy. Most of these folks 'round here call me Daddy. I wants to be your daddy, too, Chester. You's a nice lookin' boy. You sho' is. You got them pretty blue eyes, long legs, and a tight little behind. Nobody better not mess with my Chester. No, sir."

Chester, if he'd had a gun, would have put it between Daddy's eyes and pulled the trigger right then and there.

"Two ways thangs can happen for you here," Daddy said. "See, I runs this block. They don't call me Daddy for nothin'. Now, you can drop them draws you got on and let me feel around on you and get with you later on, or I can make you do it. If you do it *for* me, it'll be easier. Then, I won't let these other apes 'round here beat you with that lock in the sock you heard whirrin' about. You'll get to keep all your teeth, too, and there won't be a mark on you. You'll be Daddy's bitch and they'll know it, without me or you sayin' one word."

Again, if there was any way possible for Chester to just magically disappear into the ether, he would have gladly paid a king's ransom for it, rather than endure what was sure to come next.

"Daddy was raised in Augusta, home of James Brown, Godfather and King of Soul, God rest his sweet thing," Daddy started rattling, as if Chester actually gave a shit about his upbringing. “Daddy knows how to move and groove, and make you feel soooo sweet and good, just like one of dem bootiful songs sung by the King,” he added, as he stroked Chester’s backside.

Chester felt such revulsion at his touch, but something within him told him he’d better do what this man told him to do. He didn’t seem to have any other choice, especially since he knew the guards wouldn’t do anything about it. As scared as he was, but determined not to cry or scream, he slowly undressed for the big, yellow man.

Daddy fondled him, gazed at him, touched him on the rear, and started kissing him on the neck.

“Yeah, Chester, I’m goin’ love me some of you,” he said. “I sho’ is goin’ love me some of you.”

Daddy went over to his bunk, reached under his mattress and pulled out a condom. Then, he slid it over his rock hard erection before coming back to where Chester was standing naked as a jaybird. Gruffly bending Chester over, he started pumping and grunting. It seemed to go on for an eternity. It was painful at first, but Chester managed somehow to blot out the intense agony.

After what seemed forever and a month, words came into his mind and he recalled when he and Wanda Faye had sex in the old house back in Ludowici.

Then he heard Daddy say, “I love you, I love you, I didn’t mean to hurt you, baby. I sure do love you. You takin’ it like a man. Oh, Lord, yes. No screamin’, no cryin’, no cuttin’ up... taking it like a natural man. That’s what I loves. Smells like a man, acts like a man... Daddy’s little man. I love Daddy’s little man.”

Chester knew he had not only just heard the words, but he had spoken those same words before.

“What was it the Bible said about “your sins finding you out?” he thought.

Well, his sins had found him out and they had come home to roost. He now knew what it felt like to be a thing and not a human being.

The next morning, as he and Daddy walked down the corridor to the cafeteria for their morning meal, there were the same whoops and whirring noises coming from the other prisoners. During breakfast, however, when Daddy cut Chester’s sausage, salt and peppered his hash browns, blew on the plate to cool everything off, and then opened his milk for him, all eyes in the cafeteria could see that Daddy, indeed, had a new little man.

On the way back to the cell block, there wasn’t one taunting peep out of any of the other prisoners. Just friendly greetings.

“Hey, there, Daddy! Looking good, Daddy,

you and your little man!"

There were no more whooping sounds and no more whirring sounds... only greetings for Daddy and his little man.

Daddy was right, Chester thought later that night, as he lay in his bed praying for sleep to come soon. Neither he nor Daddy had spoken a word to a single soul, but everybody in the prison knew what was going on, even the guards.

Chapter 17

Destini's promise

A plenitude of preparations were going into the homecoming services at the House of Prayer, which kept everyone in the community busy. Over the course of the last two weeks, and being true to her word, Wanda Faye never once stopped at her mailbox.

Destini, in her ever efficient manner, placed all of Wanda Faye's mail, other than the letters from Chester, on the coffee table in Wanda Faye's living room each day. Chester's letters arrived every other day like clockwork, and with each one, his words and expressions grew angrier and angrier.

Destini, as she read each one, thought he sounded like a child telling his adversary when and what time they would meet for a fistfight.

He wrote that he would be home in Ludowici soon and then he'd be arriving in Seraph Springs to see his youngun's, and kick ass and take names if he faced any opposition. With each letter, Destini smiled bigger and bigger, as her plans were taking shape nicely.

She had recently gone down to a dentist in Gainesville where she had five of her front teeth capped with gold crowns. Carved into the gold on each tooth were letters that spelled out the name J-E-S-U-S.

"Yes, Mr. Chester Easley," she said, as she admired her teeth in the mirror. "When you see me smile at you, you're gonna see Jesus, all right, but you're gonna be in hell."

Chapter 18

The day before the homecoming service at the House of Prayer, everyone was up before the sun rose. Final preparations were being made, including dusting all the pews, setting up tables in the fellowship hall and covering them with plastic tablecloths, making sure each table had salt and pepper shakers, as well as enough chairs to seat at least 12 people each.

Outside, there was even more seating, which is where the bulk of the people would be sitting. Rawls Funeral Home in Turpricone, as they did every year, provided four tents that would offer shade from the blazing afternoon sun or, God forbid, rain, which had happened more than once in prior years.

Mr. Hamp had sent over his gigantic ice tea dispensers, as well as his hundred-cup coffeemaker the previous day. He also contacted Destini's brother, Duke, and asked him to come up from Gainesville to barbecue a whole hog and two cases of chickens. After all, nobody could barbecue like Duke. When he wasn't working for the police department in Gainesville, he'd be in Seraph Springs. On any given day you could find him at one gathering or the next around town, grilling up everything from hamburgers and hot dogs to whole hogs and deer.

Duke and his wife, Essie, had recently asked Mama Tee if they could build a house on the home place, which made her extremely happy. She gladly deeded them two acres just across the road from her. It was where the old house in which she spent her childhood had stood before it burned to the ground right before Duke was born.

Essie and Duke were both retiring from their jobs at the end of the year. Their home was already sold in Gainesville, but the new owners were allowing them to stay in it until the following Easter. They hoped to have their new house built by then, if not before. It was only a small modular home, but it would be plenty big enough to suit their needs.

Everyone in the family was overjoyed that Duke and Essie would be coming back home, however, for most of them, it seemed they had never really left.

Even Mr. Hamp told Duke not to wear himself out with all the moving preparations because he'd have some of his crew do all the heavy lifting. He also told Duke that he already had enough barbecuing and smoking jobs lined up for him to keep him busy for a long while.

Duke, it seemed, was the only person who could talk Mr. Hamp into going down to Gainesville to watch a University of Florida football game, which he did quite a few times.

Other times, Mr. Hamp would invite Duke and Essie to come to Pittstown and spend the weekend at his log cabin on the Suwannee River. He had owned it for the last twenty years, but he rarely had the time to enjoy it because he stayed so busy working seven days a week.

Duke and Essie spent much more time at the cabin than Mr. Hamp, as they were both into fishing. They were always bringing loads of fish over to Seraph Springs for everyone to enjoy at big fish fry gatherings, especially during the fall and winter months.

Tomorrow at homecoming, Duke would be outside grilling up the hog and the chickens, while Essie would be in the kitchen at the fellowship hall making her famous cheese grits and helping get the sweet iced tea just right. She loved being in the kitchen more than she did socializing. The only thing she loved more than cooking and preparing food was spending time with the children. Duke had always declared she was just a big child herself.

She took great pleasure in planning Bunnye's big birthday parties each year at Easter, too.

There was always a huge Easter egg hunt for the kids, as well as games galore to keep them occupied. She would prepare her special chicken pilau and always made certain to bake tons of Easter cakes and cupcakes. She even made Duke dress up like an Easter bunny for the parties. Even though he blustered about putting on the costume, he'd wear it and hop around in it for hours, shelling out Easter candy to all the children.

Yes, everyone in the town of Seraph Springs was busy preparing for the homecoming event.

Chapter 19

Over at the Lloyd household about one o'clock that afternoon, after lunch had been served and all the dishes had been cleaned up, Nadine and Louie, Wanda Faye, and all seven of their children were getting ready to head up to Miss Sissy's shop in Turpricone. Dink had declined the offer, saying he had his own barber he preferred.

Louie had all the kids pile into the van and he followed Wanda Faye in her pickup, where she and Nadine had some quiet time together after a busy morning getting things ready at the church for the homecoming.

When the entire crew descended upon Betty's Beauty Box, they found Miss Sissy standing in the doorway dressed in her signature gold lame smock, monogrammed with her name in big, bold letters. She hugged each and every one of them and invited them to come inside.

She had a CD playing of a well-known, local gospel vocalist, Amy Sue Swisher, who was singing, "Thank You Mama For Praying For Me".

Lollie and Mark, who were wearing identical smocks with their own names monogrammed over top of the right front pocket, were getting things ready in the shampoo room. They, too, came out to greet everyone, along with Lollie who had just returned from her lunch break.

"Come on sunshine girls and little sunbeams," Miss Sissy said, as they all followed behind her. "We need to get these handsome young men all done up first. While they're getting their hair cut, Mark, I want you take Nadine and Wanda Faye back to the manicure room and get their feet soaking in that Pedi-ready. We're gonna have them looking like movie stars tomorrow for Miss Jewell's big day. Yes, ma'am, movie stars each and ever' one of you."

It didn't take but about thirty minutes for Miss Sissy and Lollie to cut all four of the boys' hair. Lollie even gave Louie a little trim and cleaned him up some. Then, the two of them started on the three girls and had all of them trimmed in less than twenty minutes.

Louie then rounded up all the kids, said goodbye to Wanda Faye and Nadine and proceeded to head back to Seraph Springs. As they were walking out the door, the kids were asking Louie if he would stop at the Jiffy Store on the way home and buy them all an Icee.

"You betcha," he told them. "I'll even throw in

some candy and potato chips, too," he added, which was met with squeals of delight from all the kids.

Miss Sissy went to the back room where Mark was finishing up with the girls' manicures. They both had their nails done exactly the same in a deep wine color.

"What do you think, Miss Sissy?" Wanda Faye asked. "Don't they have that perfect fall look about them?"

"They certainly do," she said. "Mark, you did a fabulous job."

"Thank you, Miss Sissy," he said, blushing.

"Miss Nadine, you go on out back and smoke you one of those old cigarettes," Miss Sissy told her. "I know you're dying for a smoke. I can see it in your eyes. Meanwhile, I'll get started on Wanda Faye's hair."

"Don't mind if I do," Nadine said. "I'll be back in just a few minutes after I've had me a Vitamin N."

"A what?" Miss Sissy asked.

"Vitamin N is what she calls her cigarettes," Wanda Faye explained. "The "N" stands for nicotine."

"Oh... yeah, right," Miss Sissy said, shaking her head and laughing. "Makes sense. Take your time. I'm gonna be a little while with Wanda Faye."

While Nadine was outside, Miss Sissy began

the process of shampooing, doing the Roux rinse, the de-tangler, the rollers, and the set, and then she sat Wanda Faye down underneath the dryer.

Lollie was busy out front with an agitated customer who had just come in crying, saying she wasn't happy at all with the haircut she got at a shop on the other side of town yesterday. She looked so distraught that Lollie couldn't turn her away.

About forty-five minutes later, Miss Sissy finished up with Nadine.

"Well, I need to take me a short break," Miss Sissy said, as she stretched and yawned. "You two just relax there a while."

Both girls were sitting under the dryers in big, gold upholstered chaise lounges. There was a sign above each dryer chair that said "Her Majesty". It seemed the ladies of Turpricone had their own special effect on Miss Sissy and her choice of décor.

"You girls look just like queens on the throne," Miss Sissy said, when she came back ten minutes later. "Yes, sunshine queens... beautiful golden queens."

As if right on cue, Miss Sissy broke into her own special rendition of, "You Are My Sunshine".

"You are my sunshines, my only sunshines, you make me happy when skies are grey, you'll never know girls how much I love you, please don't take my sunshine girls away."

"That was fabulous, Miss Sissy," Mark said.

"Thank you very much," she replied, sounding a lot like Elvis Presley all of a sudden, which brought on laughter from everyone.

When Miss Sissy finished with the final spritz of hairspray on both girls' up-do's, she told them they were truly done up like Pentecostal royalty. With the aid of some wonderful hair pieces that she had special-ordered, the girls' hair reached epic heights. They could have taken the helm of most any TV evangelism show.

When she turned the two girls toward the mirror, there was a collective gasp from them both.

"Wow! We look so elegant," Nadine said.

"Oh, Miss Sissy," Wanda Faye said, in awe at her beautiful new do. "How can we ever be able to thank you?"

"Oh, Sunshine, don't think anything of it. It was my pleasure. It's been many a day since I've done so much hair in such beautiful styles. Lord, I think it was in Jackson, Mississippi some twenty-five years ago, but if I have to say so myself, the old girl's still got it."

"Yes, you do," Nadine said.

"I may have a few more miles on me than most, but I can still comb and set with the best. Now, darlings, before you go, I have a little something for you that will be the finishing touch."

Miss Sissy reached behind her styling chair

for her signature, gold lame canvas bag and brought out two boxes. Inside each box was a white enameled cross with gold trim. With all the reverence of Brother Linton as he served communion, she pinned the crosses into the front of each girl's up-swirled bun.

"There," she said. "Absolutely perfect. I knew they would be. When I saw them over in Jacksonville the other day, I knew I had to have them for you girls. Oh, Lord, I am so thankful."

"They're beautiful," Wanda Faye said, as she admired hers in the mirror.

With that, Miss Sissy lifted her hands in the air and said, "Thank you Jesus for making me your handmaiden today. Oh, praise your holy name. Glory!" she shouted, and then she danced all the way across the white tiled floor.

Minutes later, Wanda Faye and Nadine prepared to leave, while Mark cleaned up all the mess they left behind.

"Now, girls, remember to wrap those hairdos in toilet paper tonight," Miss Sissy told them. "Here's two satin pillowcases for you to put on your pillows before you go to bed."

Then, she turned to Lollie, who was standing right beside her.

"You can take their money now," Miss Sissy said. "Let's see... for all of them, let's just say five-hundred dollars, and that's with my special discount of twenty percent. With those two cans of finishing lacquer, it will come to a grand total of five-hundred-and-fifty dollars."

After Nadine settled the bill, she pulled out an envelope and a wrapped gift and handed it to Miss Sissy.

"Miss Sissy, we talked to Dee Dee and she told us this was the right thing for us to do," Nadine said. "We hope you know it is with love we give this to you."

Miss Sissy opened the envelope and inside was a card with a picture of a dove on the outside. Inside was written:

Thank you, Miss Sissy, for being so nice. Here's a tip. Take it and buy you something nice. God bless you. Your friends, Wanda Faye, Nadine and all the family.

Also inside, was a crisp one-hundred dollar bill. Miss Sissy was crying as she read the note and dabbing at her eyes. When she opened the present, more tears began to flow. Inside the box, wrapped in gold foil paper, were two of Sophie Martin's latest CD's.

"We wrapped these in gold, Miss Sissy, because we know it's your favorite color," Nadine told her. "Those CD's are because you remind us of Sophie Martin."

Miss Sissy held out her arms and hugged and kissed both girls.

"You know, darlings, I'll be at that church service tomorrow," Miss Sissy said. "Nothing could keep me from it. I'll bring my comb if y'all need a little touch up before you go in. I love you both very much. God bless you for remembering Miss Sissy. You are truly angels, my sunshine angels."

When the girls left Miss Sissy's shop, they felt as if they had already been to a revival service. They'd heard singing, shouting, some preaching, their body and spirits had received ministry, and they left a large amount in the collection plate.

Chapter 20

Destini's plot thickens

Across town on Carver Drive, Destini and Bunnye were having their hair done by Brenda Wilson, the African American cosmetologist recommended by Miss Sissy.

Destini could tell right off the bat that the girl knew what she was doing. After talking with her for a while, she learned that her grandmother, Miss Mamie, was a second cousin to Mama Tee, as both of them had been raised on Mr. Jim Campbell's farm between Seraph Springs and Turpricone.

"No wonder I like you, girl," Destini told her. "Hell, we kin."

"I guess we are," Brenda said, smiling, as she trimmed Destini's hair.

"Brenda, I want to ask you something, girl," Destini said a few minutes later. "These razors you use here at the shop, they sho' is sharp. Sharpest razors I've ever seen."

"Oh, yes," Brenda said. "Yes, ma'am, they are sharp. I special order them from up in New York."

"How much does a blade like that cost?"

"Oh, this blade, Destini, would cost you about three-hundred dollars."

Destini reached into her bosom, untied a handkerchief, and then counted out three one-hundred dollar bills and handed them to Brenda, whose eyes widened in astonishment.

"I'll order one for you, Destini," Brenda said. "You'll sure have a nice blade for keeping up yours and Bunnye's hair."

"Thank you, Brenda. I'm sho' gonna enjoy using that razor... I sho' am."

Destini couldn't stop smiling. After a few minutes, while Brenda continued working on her hair, Destini started humming a popular Aretha Franklin tune, "R-E-S-P-E-C-T".

Chapter 21

Miss Sissy cashes in

In recent weeks, the smell of all the chemicals that were used to do acrylic nails had become so noxious to Miss Sissy that she decided to remove the manicure and pedicure room from her shop altogether and simply use it for all the dryers, which she felt were too cramped in the corner. She owned the building next door and there seemed to be plenty of room for a manicure/pedicure salon.

She let it be known through an ad in the local newspaper that she wanted to rent her space next door, and for what purpose. One morning, two oriental women, who could barely speak a word of English, came by her shop. With them was an oriental man, who was a little older than the two women, and whose English was more understandable.

"Cousins learn about your shop," he said to Miss Sissy. "Want to ask you about shop."

"They're interested in my shop? Next door?" Miss Sissy asked the man. "They want to do nails?"

"Uh, yes, ma'am," he said. "Cousins want to do manicure and pedicure in your shop next door."

"Well, before I rent it to them, I want to see what they can do," Miss Sissy said, as she eyed them up and down. "Tell them to come back tomorrow and bring their manicure and pedicure sets with them. I want them to do my nails and feet. Oh, and Lollie's and Mark's, too. I want to see what they can do with the nails of both men and women."

The man nodded his head up and down, as if he understood what she was saying.

"If I give them a passing grade, I'll consider renting my shop to them," Miss Sissy continued. "If not, they can go on down the road. By the way, what is your name? And what are their names?"

Miss Sissy couldn't quite make out what he was saying, but it sounded like he said his name was Mr. Yuk. She had no clue what the names of the two women were, even though he repeated them several times.

"Well, you leave that to those who can spell it," Miss Sissy told Mr. Yuk. "I'm not going to worry with all that right now. Heck, I can't even read all that stuff on the menu over at the Red

Dragon Chinese Restaurant in Pittstown, but I love their egg rolls. I might not be able to spell their names, but I know what a good manicure and pedicure looks like."

The man tried again to pronounce their names as clearly as he could.

"It sounds like Tang and Lee to me, so that's what I'll call them, Tang and Lee," Miss Sissy said. "Tang, like the breakfast drink, and Lee, 'cause it sounds like Lee and it's pretty."

"Yes," he said, rapidly nodding his head up and down, up and down, like a yoyo.

"Tang! Lee!" Miss Sissy nearly shouted to the two women, and they both nodded, as if she got their names just right. "Good," she said. "Your cousin, Mr. Yuk, is going to bring y'all back tomorrow afternoon at five, and if I like the way you do my nails, my niece's nails, and those of our assistant, Mark, we'll talk about you maybe leasing my shop."

The two women nodded at Miss Sissy. Meanwhile, Mark was one step ahead, approaching Miss Sissy from behind.

"Here you go," he quietly said to Miss Sissy.

"Oh, yes, thank you, Mark," she said, and then she handed a signature tote bag to both women.

"Here's one for you, too, Mr. Yuk," Miss Sissy said, and then she lowered her voice and leaned in to him a little closer. "If I was you, I'd change my name. Yuk ain't such a good expression down here. By the way, where y'all from?"

"We are Vietnamese," he said. "We are from a place near Saigon. Both cousins have work visas and are working towards citizenship."

"Well," Miss Sissy said, popping her chewing gum and obviously feeling much better about the situation. "Ain't that nice? I sure am glad of that. Terrible war, terrible war. So many people lost in that war. Oh, well, we're here now, ain't we?"

"Yes, we here now," Mr. Yuk said, seemingly unfazed by her patronizing attitude.

"One thing, Mr. Yuk, over in Barkley, they's some of them folks got them little heathen temples set up with oranges and such around them and that little Buddha man," Miss Sissy started. "You tell these girls, ain't no graven images going in my shop. No Buddha and none of them little sticks burning that stuff neither... that incense stuff."

"No, ma'am," he said. "No burn stuff. No Buddhas."

"I'm a Christian woman and our customers wouldn't understand. Most of them are Baptists, Methodists, and Pentecostals, and a few Presbyterians and Episcopalians," Miss Sissy explained.

"That's what we are, my cousins and me," said Mr. Yuk.

"How's that?" Miss Sissy asked.

"That's what we are. We are Catholic," he

said. "We are not Buddhist. We went to school at a Catholic mission."

"Oh, well, that's nice. Y'all are Christians. Well, praise the Lord for that. Folks here will like that. Tell your cousins they should lay them rose beads with Jesus on the cross all around on their counters. Ain't that what y'all call them things?"

"You mean rosary beads, dear lady," Mr. Yuk corrected her.

"Yeah, that's right," Miss Sissy said. "You know, I've always thought that rosary was so pretty. I wish I could wear it around my neck, but I wouldn't feel right about it, but it is a beautiful thing. It really is."

"Well, Miss Sissy, we will see you tomorrow afternoon at five," Mr. Yuk said. "We look forward to it."

"See you then, Mr. Yuk," she said. "See you Tang and Lee."

As soon as they left, Miss Sissy turned to Mark and Lollie with a huge smile on her face.

"They sure seem like nice folks, don't they? I just know they'll do a good job, but tomorrow, I'll have to tell them about paying their rent in cash. If they ain't citizens yet, I'd be a little leery about taking a check from them. Cash will make a lot more sense, don't you think?"

"Cash always works for me," Mark said.

"Honey, cash works for anybody," Miss Sissy said. "It's a wonderful thing... good, hard, cold cash. I wonder why people call it cold cash. It sure as hell warms my heart."

The following day, Mr. Yuk, Tang and Lee arrived punctually at five o'clock. Miss Sissy showed them where to set up in the old manicure/pedicure area, and they went to work immediately. She seemed really impressed with them.

"Honey, y'all sure got some mighty pretty straight black hair," Miss Sissy said to Lee. "I got customers that would cut off their right and left boobies for pretty straight hair like yours."

Lee just smiled and continued working on Miss Sissy's manicure.

"God bless her, she don't understand nothin', nothin' at all," Miss Sissy said to Mark, who was sitting beside her getting his manicure done by Tang. "She's like ol' lady Brouchard, who comes in here from over in Bristol Park. That poor soul can't hear thunder when it's right over her head. I gotta shout everything to her, and then she just smiles and nods her head. Her being hard of hearing ain't got nothin' to do with her pocketbook, though. Just 'cause her ears are broke, don't mean she is," she added.

Mr. Yuk was sitting nearby taking everything in and making sure the two women were doing a good job.

"Mr. Yuk, I hope you're gonna be in that shop helping these girls understand English for a while," Miss Sissy said. "We don't want them to be cheated, and I sure don't want to be cheated."

"Oh, not to worry, I will be in there with them all the time, but they are learning faster than you can imagine," Mr. Yuk assured her.

As Lee was putting the final coat on Miss Sissy's fingernails, she looked up at her.

"You want jail on nail?" she asked.

"What's that, honey? No, baby. Ain't nobody going to no jail. She don't think she's going to jail, does she, Mr. Yuk?"

"Miss Sissy, she want to know if you want her to put jeweled design on fingernails," Mr. Yuk explained, as he attempted not to laugh.

"Ohhhh... tell her, yes, ma'am, the works," Miss Sissy said, as her face turned a bright shade of red. "I especially love butterflies."

By the time Lee finished, Miss Sissy's nails were beautifully polished with jeweled butterflies encrusted on pink roses on both her pinky and index fingers.

"Now, this is a work of art," Miss Sissy said. "A divine work of art. This is absolutely beautiful."

Lee smiled at her and so did Mr. Yuk, while Miss Sissy and Mark were admiring her handiwork.

"I can't wait for her to do me up for Christmas with candy canes, and holly with gold leaves, maybe even some little bells or a Santa Claus head," Miss Sissy started rambling. "Oh, I do love Christmas. I sure do."

A short time later, after inspecting Lollie and Mark's manicures and pedicures, Miss Sissy brought out a prepared contract that Carl Alvin had drawn up for her and she presented it to Mr. Yuk.

"Y'all sure are talented girls, and I wish you all the best," she said to the two women. "I really do. Now, Mr. Yuk, have the girls sign right there by the big red X. They'll need to sign in English, too."

After the women signed the contract, Mr. Yuk handed it back to Miss Sissy.

"Thank you very much, Mr. Yuk. Y'all can give me my thousand dollar security deposit before you leave. I'll be around on the last Friday of each month for my rent."

Mr. Yuk handed Miss Sissy a bank envelope that contained ten crisp hundred dollar bills. Miss Sissy's eyes lit up as she counted out the money. Then, she had Mark write them a receipt.

"It sure is nice doing business with you folks. It sure is," Miss Sissy said.

As soon as they left, Miss Sissy turned to Mark and she had the biggest smile on her face.

"It takes all kinds to make up the world, but ain't they nice people?" she asked him. "And they sure know how to work and count money. Hell, they're on their way to success, I'd say."

Chapter 22

Homecoming Sunday at the House of Prayer in Seraph Springs was a picture-perfect fall day on the banks of the Suwannee River. The goldenrods, the Indian paint brushes, even the wild coreopsis that most folks mistakenly referred to as Black-eyed Susan's, were scattered around in large areas of the flat woods in and around the entire community. Today, their colors seemed much more vibrant.

Wanda Faye and Nadine had utilized all the wildflower colors to decorate the church and the fellowship hall. They even purchased new dresses with beautiful fall prints for this special occasion.

Their mama, an expert seamstress, made a suit for herself out of a deep purple material that was very becoming on her.

"You look like a queen in your royal purple outfit, Mama," Wanda Faye told her.

"I feel like a queen today," Miss Jewell said. "When I look out and see my two girls, my son-in-law, my son-in-law to be, my precious grandchildren, and my sweet Destini and Bunnye, I tell you it's a blessed day today. Thank you, Lord, Jesus."

As the service began inside the sanctuary, Brother Linton welcomed everyone and led them in prayer. Then, he asked Wanda Faye and Nadine to come to the podium. As they rose from their seats, the two girls grabbed Destini's hands and brought her with them up to where Brother Linton was standing.

"Destini is our third sister," Nadine said into the microphone. "Don't we all look alike?" she asked the congregation, which prompted a few chuckles from the crowd.

Destini had been giving speeches in churches since she was Bunnye's age, so she took the lead, in what the girls referred to as her official voice. Gone was any semblance of the local dialect, as each word she spoke was enunciated clearly and distinctly.

"Brothers and sisters in Jesus, this is the day that the Lord has made. Let us rejoice and be glad in it," she began. "To Brother Linton, members of the clergy, honored guests, and ladies and gentleman, for those of you who don't know me, my name is Destini Wilson. I have been attending this church off and on my entire life. I think the first time Mama Tee brought me here I was just a baby. Miss Jewell held me during most of the service, because I fell asleep in her arms.

Dear friends, for all these years, these two ladies, my sisters Nadine and Wanda Faye, have been held up by the arms of a woman who is wonderful in every way, and that is you, Miss Jewell."

After many hearty "Amen's" from the crowd, Destini continued.

"Now, I won't lie to you, folks. When we were growing up, there were times I didn't like Miss Jewell a whole lot, especially when she'd swing that switch and bring it across our legs when we done mischief. I have to tell you, though, she did it because she loved us. While I may not have liked the whippings, Miss Jewell, I loved you then and I still love you today."

More "Amen's" were shouted from the crowd and when the audience quieted down, Destini spoke again.

"Miss Jewell has raised two beautiful daughters, and as part of her legacy, she has a wonderful son-in-law. Stand up back there, Louie!" Destini shouted. "She also has seven grandchildren. There's Little Chet, Victor Newman, Dale Earnhardt, Charlene and Darlene, John Lewis, Jewell Lee, and I'm going to name number eight, my own baby, Easter Bunnye. There's also a future son-in-law. Stand up Dink, so they can all see you! Ain't he pretty?"

Dink was clearly embarrassed and simply waved his hand to the crowd, rather than stand up, but he received loud applause from everyone, just the same.

"Now, Miss Jewell," Destini said. "Through all the years I've known you, you've had one constant friend whom you talked to on a daily basis, confided in, laughed with, and cried with, and, yes, argued with," she added, smiling. "If the two of you weren't talking about taking a meal to a sick brother or sister in the church, you were arguing about the refreshments at the Bible Drill. It's been the same and hasn't changed all these years. Those of you who are here today know who I'm talking about, and that's Sister Velma."

Again, there was more applause and more "Amen's", as Sister Velma and Miss Jewell, who were sitting side by side, hugged one another.

"About the only time in my life I've ever seen these two women even close to resting, and it's still the same today, is when they're watching Reverend Lenny Lister on television. They do love that man and his puffy hairdo," she said, which prompted laughter from the congregation. "Even when they were supposed to be resting while watching Brother Lucius, they were usually shelling peas or doing needlework or something. Usually, that big old green and white sewing basket of Miss Jewell's would be on the floor beside her and she'd be sewing on something or other. The same with Sister Velma. Come on, you two. Get on up here."

When the "Amen's" and clapping subsided,

and Sister Velma regained her composure, Destini put her arms around the two ladies.

"Wanda Faye and Nadine, y'all come over here, too," Destini said, as she choked back tears. "I'm gonna let you take it over now."

"Mama, Sister Velma," Nadine began. "Me and Louie had some good fortune not too many months ago when his injury case was settled by Carl Alvin Campbell. Carl Alvin's in the back there with his uncle, Mr. Hamp Brayerford. They've both been wonderful friends to us and to this church. Mama, Sister Velma, I knew y'all wouldn't let me buy you new dresses or take you for a day of shopping in Jacksonville, or even out to eat at a nice restaurant. You would have both told me not to waste my money. You keep saying you're old and old folks don't need much, but me, Wanda Faye and Destini decided this time, like so many times in the past, we weren't gonna listen to you. Except today, I hope y'all don't whip us," she added.

There was a collective hush across the pews, as everyone waited for Nadine to continue.

"Mama, Sister Velma, we'd like to present you with an all-expense-paid, two-week trip to the Holy Land with Brother Lenny Lister," Nadine announced.

Everyone in the audience gasped.

"You leave two weeks from tomorrow," Nadine told them. "You'll walk where Jesus walked.

I know it's been a lifetime dream of yours, and today it's coming true."

Miss Jewell and Sister Velma were holding onto each other, crying tears of joy and utter surprise. Throughout the sanctuary, shouts of the faithful echoed, "Glory, glory, hallelujah and Amen!"

As Sister Mary Leigh played the introduction to the hymn, "Softly and Tenderly" on the piano, the entire congregation joined in to sing each verse.

Wanda Faye was taken by complete surprise when Dink got up from his seat and came up to the altar. Following behind him were their four children. As if on cue, right behind them was Louie and the Lloyd's three children. Trailing just a few steps behind was little Bunnye.

"Brother Linton," Dink said, after the song ended. "Me and Louie talked it over last night, and we've also had many conversations out at Camp EZ. Louie is already a part of Miss Jewell's family, and me and Wanda Faye's gonna be married here in a few weeks, God willing. I ain't never joined the church and never spoke in front of a crowd of people, but we want the whole family, all of us, to be on the right road, as we give thanks to the Lord for being so good and kind to us."

You could have heard a pin drop in the church, except for the soft playing of the piano.

Wanda Faye, Nadine and Destini quickly gathered around their loved ones, as Dink found the Lord, and the children and Louie all rededicated themselves to God.

Suddenly, Sister Velma lifted both hands toward heaven and yelled, "Jesus!"

Then, she fainted on the floor next to the podium. Miss Jewell and Sister Mary Lee rushed to her side. They were on either side of her, softly whispering, "Help her, sweet Jesus. Oh, Lord Jesus, yes."

Brother Linton grabbed a white coverlet from behind the piano and spread it across Sister Velma's legs, as her dress had flown up when she fainted. Then, he snatched some smelling salts from the pulpit and waved it under her nose trying to awaken her.

Sister Velma soon opened her eyes and then rose up to a standing position, slowly regaining her composure.

Miss Jewell shouted, "Glory, glory to God! Oh praise the holy name of Jesus!" Then she yelled something that sounded like, "Hallow, wallow, sheem, sheem!"

When she started dancing on one foot across the stage, everyone in the audience began chanting, "Amen, amen, amen," as hair pins began shooting out from Miss Jewell's head every which way.

It was an odd scene, but everyone seemed to

take it in stride. Once Miss Jewell quieted down and stopped dancing, she went over to where Brother Linton and Sister Velma were standing behind the pulpit.

"What I'd like to request now is a time at this altar for prayer and thanksgiving," Miss Jewell said, in a calm, serene voice.

Many in the audience joined them by the altar and got down on their knees, as Brother Linton prayed.

"Thank you, Lord Jesus, for this blessed day and for these blessed girls who have made two of our flock so happy today," he began. "I know, Lord, joy bells in heaven are ringing, and we thank you, Lord, that we lived to witness this. It is such a wonderful and happy occasion. Now, Lord, we pray for these, your servants. Bless and keep them, Lord. Be with them as they go to walk where you walked. Lord, I was going to preach a full sermon today, but your spirit is so powerful in this little house today, Lord, that I can't say anymore. So, all I am going to do now is bless the wonderful food we will have in the fellowship hall, and say thank you for the wonderful hands that prepared it. And, Lord, as we leave this sanctuary today, I am going to ask Sister Mary Lee to play, "He Set Me Free" on the piano. I want us all to sing it like we mean it in our hearts, and greet each other before we go out with genuine Christian love."

As Sister Mary Lee played the introduction, the bass guitarist and drummer joined in, as well as the electric guitar player. The entire congregation began to sing.

Once like a bird in prison I dwelt,
No freedom from my sorrow I felt,
But Jesus came and listened to me,
And glory to God, He set me free.

As the congregation eased into the second verse, there was a great deal of hugging, kissing, hand-shaking, and patting on the back.

As everyone was leaving for the fellowship hall, Wanda Faye glanced at the souvenir hand fans that she and Nadine had printed for the occasion. On the back was written, "It's been good to be in the house of the Lord."

"How true," she thought, and she smiled and silently prayed.

Dink came over to her and put his arm around her shoulder. The weighted down, bad feeling she'd had earlier in the week was nearly gone now. There was still a little bit of something there nagging at her, though, and she couldn't quite pinpoint what it could be. As she gazed into Dink's eyes, she wondered if Miss Margot or even Sophie Martin had ever been this happy.

Chapter 23

At the airport in Jacksonville, Wanda Faye and Nadine laughed until they cried when their mama tried repeatedly to make it through the security scanner. Each time she went through, the buzzer went off. Even a handheld scanner they used on her kept going off and it was always when they put it near her head.

Finally, an airport security officer named Hank, figured out it was the multitude of hair pins she used to hold up the big bun on top of her head. When Sister Velma came through and the same buzzing started, Hank simply motioned her through.

"Lady, I've had enough prayers from Mrs. Lee here to last me a lifetime," Hank said. "And, no ma'am, I don't need any more religious pamphlets. Mrs. Lee gave me four, but, thank you."

"Well, I'll be," Sister Velma said, shaking her head, as they continued into the terminal.

A good hour-and-a-half later, Wanda Faye and Nadine waved goodbye to their mama and

Sister Velma. Wanda Faye, for one, knew the Holy Land would never be the same after their visit.

"If the President put Mama and Sister Velma at the table to negotiate Middle Eastern peace, there's no doubt in my mind it would be accomplished," Wanda Faye said to Nadine, as they began the long walk back out of the terminal.

"You got that right," Nadine agreed, laughing. "By the time Mama would wear everyone down with memorizing Bible verses, and Sister Velma stopped praying over them after anointing them with oil, there'd be peace in the Middle East and it would be on their terms."

That morning, before they left the house to go to the airport, Wanda Faye had asked her mother about the small, white Bible she carried down the aisle on her wedding day, and if it would be okay if she used it, too.

Her mother told her she was welcome to use it, but that it was packed away with a lot of other things in an old tobacco pack house behind her home, and that she would need to go through all the boxes to find it.

Impatient as she could be at times, Wanda Faye decided to look for it herself. The following Saturday morning, she, Dink and the children drove over to her mama's house right after breakfast.

Wanda Faye parked the kids in front of the television to watch cartoons in the den, while she and Dink began their search for the little, white Bible.

The aroma of dried tobacco still lingered inside the old pack house, even though it had been many years since the place had been in operation. Wanda Faye could still visualize all the piles of chopped heart pine that were used as a starter fuel, which the locals referred to as lightard.

A thin layer of dust and more than a few cobwebs lay atop and around most of the big items inside the building, as well as the dozens and dozens of boxes that were stacked one atop the other. In her mother's fastidious way, though, the majority of it was covered with old burlap tobacco sheets and old bedspreads, quilts and blankets.

As Wanda Faye rooted through the first box she opened, she found the baby books her mother had kept for her and Nadine. She also found their old teddy bears, rattles and children's storybooks.

"Mama never threw anything away," she said to Dink, laughing.

Dink had just opened another box, and then another and another. Inside all three large boxes there must have been over a hundred clean, glass mason jars. Many of them still had gold caps on them, although, they had rusted with age.

"Those would make wonderful vases for wildflowers for the rehearsal supper at Camp EZ, wouldn't they, honey?" she asked Dink.

"Yeah, I guess so," he said. "What's that over there? That big black thing?"

He pointed to the back corner of the building where there was a crib, an old baby swing and a huge antique stroller.

"It's a perambulator, as Mama used to call it," she said. "Mr. Hamp ordered it for her from England right before I was born. Mama said she was always a little embarrassed pushing around such a big, expensive baby carriage in Seraph Springs. She said she only did it because Mr. Hamp put a lot of thought into the gift and really wanted her to have it," she explained. "She used to have pictures around the house with me and Nadine lying in it and..."

"Okay, enough reminiscing, Wanda Faye," Dink said, cutting her off. "We came out here on a mission to find something and we still got lots of boxes to go through."

"Yes, I know, I know," she said with a heavy sigh. "Oh, look at this. It's marked school items," she said, as she opened another box. Dink just shook his head and tore into some more boxes.

Inside Wanda Faye's box were old report cards, class photos, a couple of annuals from high school, science fair ribbons, certificates for perfect attendance for both her and Nadine, as well as ribbons from all the Bible Drills she and her sister attended as children.

Twenty minutes later, in a box marked "personal", Wanda Faye finally found the little, white Bible. The box also held some black and white photos of her parents on the day they got married at the House of Prayer. As she browsed through them, she thought how young and full of promise they both looked.

"Look, honey, look at Mama with her long, black hair. She looks like a movie star," she said, as Dink came and sat down beside her.

Miss Jewell was dressed in a beautiful white suit, matching hat, and gloves that went all the way up past her elbows. Around her neck was a gold cross necklace, a gift from her daddy to her on their wedding day. She still wore that necklace and, as far as Wanda Faye knew, had never taken it off.

"Look, Dink!" she said. "There in her hands. It's the little, white Bible."

Pinned on top of it, was the prettiest white orchid Wanda Faye had ever seen.

"Grandma Thomas had that orchid fixed on it for Mama," she said. "She told me and Nadine the story at least a hundred times when we were growing up."

Wanda Faye then explained how her parents met. She said they had known each other all their lives and rode the same school bus together, but they never courted until he came back on leave from the Army, which he had joined after he graduated from high school.

"Mama was sixteen years old, and he saw her at a Wednesday night prayer meeting," Wanda Faye explained. "He told his sister, Mama's best friend, Aunt Magdalene, that he thought Mama was the prettiest girl he'd ever seen, and that he was going to marry her. The following week, he came to her parent's house and asked for permission to call on her. Mama said her daddy, Grandpa Thomas, gave his permission, but told him that for the first month their dates would be restricted to seeing each other at home or at church."

"Pretty strict, huh?" Dink asked.

"Maybe just a little," Wanda Faye said, laughing. "He said she was smart and that until she had that high school diploma in her hand, she wasn't gonna marry him or nobody else."

"I guess they waited, huh?" Dink asked.

"Yep, they waited, but not very long. The Saturday after Mama graduated from high school, they got married in the House of Prayer."

Dink just laughed.

"Grandma Thomas saved her money from selling eggs for four weeks to buy Mama that white orchid that was pinned on her Bible," Wanda Faye continued. "It also served as the corsage on her going away suit."

As Wanda Faye held the little, white Bible in her hands, she could actually hear her mother telling the story.

"Grandma Thomas had your granddaddy take her over to Pittstown a good two months before the wedding, and she talked to the lady, Miss Mary Meadows at Mary's Flowers. That was the only florist in Pittstown at the time.

Way back then, that orchid corsage cost fifteen dollars, and that was a lot of money in those days for one flower with a little net and ribbon around it, but Grandma Thomas was determined.

She kept my little white Bible that was given to her by her preacher, old Reverend John Jonas, when I was born, and she took it out right before my wedding and had Miss Mary fix the orchid on it.

We didn't have a store bought wedding cake. Miss Mary Lee's mama made three big, white pound cakes and iced them in white. Then, she took red roses from her running rose bushes and put them on top of the cakes.

We had mints, nuts, and your grandma worked for weeks making cheese straws. The ladies of the church made that green wedding punch. I still love it today.

If any of you girls ever have a church wedding, I want you to use this little, white Bible, and I'll have a white orchid put on top of it, just like my mama did for me."

Unfortunately, Wanda Faye and Nadine

didn't get married in the church, but in front of a judge. So, until today, the little, white Bible had rested safely in its box.

Wanda Faye and Dink were about to go round up the kids and head back home when Dink spotted something.

"What's in them boxes on top of that table way over there in the corner with the tobacco sheets thrown over 'em?" he asked.

"Oh, probably old iced tea glasses or dishes," Wanda Faye said. "Or it could be more Bible Drill stuff. Mama's been storing it for over thirty years, you know. Just leave that old mess alone."

"No!" Dink said in a defiant tone. "If it's some of your daddy's old tools in them boxes, I'm gonna ask Miss Jewell if I can buy 'em from her. She may not want to part with 'em, but I'm gonna ask her just the same."

"I don't think them's Daddy's things, Dink. Most of Daddy's old tools are out in the shop where he used to work on the pulpwood trucks. They're lined up on the wall, just as neat as they were the day he died."

"Well, I'm gonna look anyway, Wanda Faye," he said. "You act like you don't want me to see what's over there. You would think you was trying to hide somethin' from me."

"Dink!" she yelled, as he hurried over to the mysterious boxes. "I told you I don't know what's in them things. Why don't we just go? We found what we was lookin' for."

Dink wasn't dissuaded in the least. He seemed determined to find out what was in the boxes, whether Wanda Faye approved or not. After he yanked the burlap tobacco sheets off, he saw the box tops were taped shut, unlike the rest of the boxes in the building. On the sides of each of the four boxes was written in bold, black letters the word "Junk".

"That's strange," Dink said, as Wanda Faye came up beside him. "I ain't seen not one box in all these we opened that was labeled "Junk", and yet, here's four boxes of 'em. If it's really junk, then why are they taped up so good?"

When Wanda Faye saw the handwriting, she knew it wasn't her mother's. It was Chester's as sure as it was anybody's. She knew his handwriting better than her own. Her mouth went dry and she suddenly felt nauseous. That bad feeling she had the other day surged into her head, into her stomach, and every part of her being.

The tops of the boxes were triple-taped with three-inch wide masking tape. Dink grabbed each one of them and set them on the floor. Then, he grabbed his pocket knife and cut the masking tape down the center of each one.

When he opened the first box, Wanda Faye thought she was going to pass out, like she'd seen her mama and Sister Velma do so many times in church. Inside the box, packed as tightly as possible, were stacks and stacks of hundred dollar bills.

"Oh, God, Dink," Wanda Faye gasped. This is what Chester was talking about in that letter."

"What letter, Wanda Faye? You and Chester been writin' each other?"

"Oh, God... no, Dink! I wanted to tell you, but Destini made me swear not to worry you with it. I thought I was doing right. Now, I see I was wrong. I should have told you, I know."

"Told me what?" Dink asked, clearly agitated now.

"Chester's been threatening me," she said. "He's been tellin' me about comin' down here tryin' to see the youngun's, and even threatening to hurt you. I was so scared I didn't know what to do. Destini told me she'd take care of everything. I ain't answered him one time, not one time, Dink. It's you I love, honey. It's you I've always loved, and *will* always love. Please believe me, Dink."

"What about all this money?" he asked her. "Look at it! Before we leave here, we're gonna count this damned money."

For nearly an hour, she and Chester had quietly and methodically counted all the bills. When they finished their calculations, they were both astonished to find there was about nine-hundred-fifty-five thousand dollars total in all four of the cardboard boxes.

"Now, Wanda Faye," Dink said, more than a little perturbed by this point. "Maybe you could give me nine-hundred-fifty-five thousand reasons why I should trust you."

"Dink, honey, I know this looks bad. It is bad, but I didn't know a thing about it. If you'll give me your cell phone, I'll call Destini and have her come out here to explain things."

"Go ahead and call her. You might as well call Nadine, too. Hell, the three Musketeers together!" he shouted. "All for one, and one for all? Is that it, Wanda Faye? Put all your trust in them, but keep the man you love in the dark? It don't make sense to me, and it hurts me. More than that, I'm disappointed, Wanda Faye. I'm disappointed that you wouldn't tell me about the trouble you was havin'."

"I was afraid you'd want to do something crazy, Dink, and right now, you're thinking something crazy, I'm sure. I can't lose you, Dink. I lost you for over ten years and I can't lose you again."

"Why not, Wanda Faye? What would be so terrible about me going on my way now? You're in school, you got good support with the girls and your mama..." he trailed off.

"Dink, you're acting like a baby, now. You are. You're the most important person in the world to me. Again, I didn't know anything about this money. I know now that Chester put it here. I also know Mama let him put it here, but I'm certain she didn't have any idea what it was. I know he told her something about them missions and missionaries he was always talkin' about. Mama always thought Chester was wonderful because he played the bass guitar in the church, and he knew the words to most of them old hymns she loves."

"What are you gonna do about this money?" Dink asked. "This is a pile of money, Wanda Faye! We could do a lot with this!"

"We're calling the sheriff and we're turning this money over to him, Dink," she adamantly said. "This is drug money and we're gonna do the right thing."

Just as Wanda Faye was about to call Destini, she and Nadine came rolling up the drive in Destini's old black pickup. As they walked over to the pack house, Destini started shouting as loud as she could.

"Any blaming to be done here, Dink, put it on me!" she screamed, and then she lowered her voice when she entered the pack house. "Wanda Faye wanted to tell you, but I made her swear not to say anything. Here's the letters," she added, and handed a bundle of them to Dink.

"How did you know we were here, Destini?" Wanda Faye asked.

"I knows ever'thing," was all she said.

Dink sat down in an old lawn chair under the shelter of the pack house and started reading the letters, while the girls sat and watched his reactions. His face turned beet red and Wanda Faye could swear she saw smoke coming out of his ears.

"I'll kill him!" Dink yelled. "I'll kill him! I swear, I'll kill that bastard! Lord help me!" He then turned to Wanda Faye. "Honey, forgive me," he said. "Can you forgive me?"

As quick as she could, she ran to him and put her arms around his neck, holding him tight.

"There's nothing to forgive, Dink," she said. "You don't have to ask forgiveness when you love somebody. What was that line in that sad show, *Love Story*, when that pretty dark-haired girl who dies at the end tells her man that love means never having to say you're sorry? Well, if it's true love, she's right, and Dink, I truly love you."

Nadine, meanwhile, had taken it upon herself to call Sheriff Lewis. Within minutes, he was pulling up to the pack house. He took statements from Dink and from Wanda Faye, and said he'd have to wait until Miss Jewell got back to take her statement.

"Unfortunately, Wanda Faye, this won't change a thing about Chester's release," Sheriff Lewis told her. "A man can't be tried twice for the same thing. I wish I could tell you different, but I can't. This may help our investigation, though, and give us some new insights about all the drug trafficking that's been goin' on around here."

“So, that makes about two million dollars they made off sellin’ drugs,” Wanda Faye said, shaking her head in disbelief. “They already recovered close to a million already when Chester was first arrested.”

“Yep, they had a thriving business goin’ on,” Sheriff Lewis said. “I’ll keep my eye on Chester, honey. I got connections up in Georgia. Chester will still be on probation when he gets out, you know. He better walk the straight chalk line or he’ll be right back behind them bars.”

“Thank you, Sheriff Lewis,” Wanda Faye said.

“Thank you for calling me,” he replied. “It was the right thing to do. I’ll be back ‘round with y’all about the reward. I’m sure there’ll be one of some kind or other.”

As the sheriff was pulling out of the drive, Destini started mumbling under her breath, but it was loud enough that Wanda Faye overheard her.

“Ain’t gonna be no worries ‘bout Chester,” Destini muttered, shaking her head from side to side. “Chester, Chester, Mr. Pester, ain’t gonna be pesterin’ much more. No, ma’am.”

Chapter 24

Chester Easley's worst nightmare

"You mine! You my man! Don't matter where you go, you mine! I'm be coming to you soon, 'cause I loves you! You can't get away from Daddy! Daddy knows all 'bout where you is!"

Chester kept hearing the words over and over in his head on the bus ride from the prison in upstate Georgia down to Albany. Daddy had screamed those words over and over and over while Chester was walking down the cell block on his way out to freedom.

Daddy screamed those words for so long and so loud that he became hoarse after a while. Finally, the prison guards, six of them, had to subdue him. They even had to summon the nurse from the infirmary to come and give him a strong sedative, Deputy Fleming told him later.

Even after Daddy's screams stopped, Chester could hear all the whooping sounds, as the other inmates gave him the grand send-off. This time there were no whirring noises, those dreaded sounds caused by a steel lock tied up in the end of a sock. Now, it was just a steady whoop, whoop, whoop, interspersed with Daddy's little man, bye-bye Daddy's baby, Daddy's comin' for you, can't get away from Daddy.

As he sat alone on the back seat of the bus, Chester closed his eyes, but he couldn't go to sleep. All he could see was Daddy pounding on the jail cell, screaming those words again and again and again.

In his pocket, he had a bottle of sleeping pills that were given to him by the prison doctor upon his release.

"You may need these," the doctor had told him. "I've had so many inmates return to this prison who told me they could never really go to sleep. This is a prescription called Ambien and it may cause hallucinations, or maybe not. You'll sleep, though. Just don't be alarmed when those hallucinations start. It's only a temporary thing."

Chester vowed he wouldn't take any of the pills until he reached Ludowici and his grandma's old house, and he stuck to it.

Hours later, right before midnight, the Greyhound pulled into the bus station on the outskirts of Albany. Using part of the twenty bucks he got from the prison as a going away present, he hailed a cab to take him to Ludowici, which was about ten miles to the south. He asked the cabbie to drop him off at Miss Alma Ruth's Café, hoping it might be open so he could grab a bite to eat. When he got there, though, it was closed.

Chester's grandmother's house was just across the highway and it looked mighty good, he thought, cheerful even, with a new coat of green paint. After so many years staring at the dark grey walls of prison, anything with a little color to it looked good now. Someone had even cleaned up the yard and fixed the two busted windows in the living room.

After retrieving the key from under a planter on the back porch, he went back around and unlocked the front door. He flipped on a light switch in the kitchen and was pleased to find out the electric was turned on at the old place.

He had been writing the preacher at the Ludowici House of Prayer, who told him the congregation agreed to clean up the place and turn the power on for him. One of the church members had an old window air conditioner and even installed it in the bedroom for him.

He was glad he kept up his correspondence with his friends at the church. He wished with all his might, however, that he had never written Wanda Faye all those letters. He didn't mean most of what he had written. All he wanted was to hold her just once more and tell her how sorry he was for the way he treated her.

He knew now, after three years of systematic physical and mental abuse from Daddy, what it was like to feel alone and hopeless, and to know the awful dread of facing yet another round of abuse each and every day.

He had confided to the prison psychiatrist about his upbringing, and the doctor told him his grandmother was, without a doubt, a woman with emotional challenges that manifested themselves in cruelty. He told Chester that while this was no excuse for the way he treated Wanda Faye, it was, at least, a partial explanation of why.

It also explained to Chester why he so easily gave in to Daddy. It was to avoid more pain. The one time he tried to avoid the scrubbing of his hands with lye water, his grandma stripped him naked, beat him, and made him stand in a foot tub of hot lye water until he screamed in agony. He still had one toenail that never grew back as a result of that scalding.

As he meandered through the house, he breathed in the air, which was scented with Pine Sol, and then he smelled the fabric softener that had been used on the sheets in the bedroom. It was a far cry from the awful stench inside the prison.

On the oil cloth-covered dining room table was a card. When he opened it, he found a picture of Jesus praying in the garden on the outside. Written on the inside was a long message.

Dear Brother Chester, welcome home. We, your church family at the House of Prayer are here for you.

You will find ham and a bowl of potato salad, as well as a bowl of banana pudding in the refrigerator. There is also a loaf of fresh bread, a big jar of mayonnaise and a small jar of mustard, as well as a head of lettuce, a jar of dill pickles, and a package of cheese slices, if you want to make a sandwich.

We also left you a half gallon of sweet milk, a dozen eggs and a pound of butter. We left a new shaker of salt and pepper, and some cooking oil for you by the stove. There is a can of coffee and a container of sugar by the coffeemaker.

On your nightstand, we left you a brand new Bible with your name engraved in gold. Everyone deserves a fresh start and we thought a new Bible would be good for you.

We also had your electric bass guitar refurbished and tuned. She's ready to go for you, and we're ready to hear you play.

We'll see you soon, once you settle in. Rest well. May Jesus be with you and bless you with a good night's sleep. With our love and prayers, your church family, Ludowici House of Prayer.

Chester had lost his appetite and, quite frankly, he was too tired now to fix anything to eat. Instead, he poured a glass about half full of milk, took a sip, then swallowed two of the sleeping pills and downed them with the remainder of the milk. The prescription said to only take one pill, but he wanted so much to just sleep the whole night through.

"Heck, if one of these can put me to sleep, two should put me out dead to the world," he thought.

Even though it was early October, it was still quite warm inside the house, so he turned the window unit on and switched it to the low cool setting. He stripped off his clothes and lay naked on the bed, nodding off a few minutes later.

Throughout the night, Chester was haunted by all sorts of dreams, but it was the nightmarish one just before daybreak that brought him to his knees with fear.

He awoke suddenly about four in the morning when he felt something cold and sharp resting against his testicles. He broke out in a cold sweat and kept his eyes clammed shut, certain he was going to hear the words, "Daddy is here. I tol' you, I ain't never givin' you up."

At first, all he heard was heavy breathing. As he slowly opened his eyes in the semi-darkened room, he saw what looked to be a black person with some sort of stocking over their head. He couldn't make out the person's features, but he sure did see the straight razor that was resting against his balls. He could see that clear as day.

He soon began to feel quick little scratches

against the tender skin, and then the unmistakable feel of warm blood oozing down between his thighs.

He knew he was conscious, but he couldn't seem to do or say anything. Looking down toward his groin, he watched a black hand with a straight razor make quick, rapid nicks all over the inside of his thighs.

"Oh, Jesus! Oh, Lord, have mercy!" he cried out. "Please tell Daddy I'm being good! I ain't being unfaithful! Tell Daddy I won't never try to leave him! I promise! Oh, don't cut me anymore! I'm begging you!"

"Begging? You begging?" a husky voice asked him. "Something new for you to beg, ain't it Mr. Man? I don't know who yer daddy is, whether you be talkin' 'bout Jesus or your own daddy, but right now, this nigger with the razor is Mama, Daddy, everybody else to you. You hear me?"

"Oh, God, yes, please, please!" Chester cried.

"This is the real shit here, Mr. Chester Easley," the voice continued. "I'm your worst damned nightmare. A mean nigger with a straight razor and you better hear what I'm fixin' to tell you, boy. You better listen to me real good. Are you listening, boy?"

The straight razor was now at the base of the shaft of his flaccid penis and could, with one slight movement of the hand, slice off his manhood. That, he knew for sure. His mouth was full of bile and a cold sweat enveloped his nakedness.

"This is worse than prison," he wildly thought.

He was supposed to be a free man now, but this was a jail worse than any godforsaken penitentiary.

"I hear you," he said to the voice. "I'm listening. Oh, Lord, I'll do anything. Please, I beg you, don't kill me. Please don't kill me."

"Here's the message, boy. Quit writin' letters to your ex wife. She's real upset and that causes others to get upset, like me. Quit callin' her, and don't make no effort to come below that state line. 'Cause if you do, I'm here to tell you, boy, next time, you'll see them little marbles you calls nuts, and that little pencil you call a dick, sliced off and thrown on the floor! Then, I'll cut you from A to Izzum before I finish your ass off. You hear me good, boy!"

There was a brief silence. All Chester could hear was the sound of his heart pounding through his skull.

"This nightmare nigger goin' leave now. You better lie on that bed and not even try to get up to piss, until you see the sun shining bright outside that window. Don't worry 'bout that money you hid in Florida, neither. It's gone, found and turned into the law. Gone, gone, boy."

Again, there was another moment of silence. All Chester could hear was more heavy breathing coming from atop where he lay.

"Everything down there gone and dead to you, but you alive, and if you wanna stay alive, stay in Georgia or north of the state line, 'cause the minute you hit it, I'll know. Yes, sir, and I'll come again in the darkness and kill you graveyard dead."

"I promise, I promise!" Chester cried.

"No phone calls, no messages, boy," the voice continued. "Let's just say, to coin a phrase you crackers love, that I done vanished like a nigger in the night. Close your eyes tight now, boy, just like you goin' to sleep, and don't open them eyes for a good long while. I'll be watching you, yes, I will be, boy."

Chester tightly closed his eyes and he felt the weight lift off his body. The voice was gone and then there was complete silence. Hot tears oozed from his eyes and he silently prayed.

"Oh, save me, dear, Jesus. Help me, oh, Lord, save me."

Over and over, he prayed and then he drifted off to sleep again. The next thing he heard was the old game rooster crow that lived in the yard across the road at Miss Etta Maye's Diner, and he opened his eyes. He saw that his bed sheet was wet with sweat and blood.

"What the hell?" he gasped, as he looked down between his legs. "Jesus, God! If this is what hallucinations do to you, I ain't takin' anymore of them damn pills!"

He slowly got up, grunting and groaning in pain as he did so, and went into the bathroom. In the light he could see dried blood all over his groin area. After grabbing a wash cloth, he dampened it with warm water and lightly dabbed at the nicks on his inner thighs, as well as the two small ones on his scrotum.

He opened the medicine cabinet and snatched a bottle of hydrogen peroxide. Then, he poured the liquid all over his groin, screaming in agony as he did so. There was a tube of antibiotic salve on the shelf, so he gently applied it to all the nicks on his skin until the bulk of the pain subsided.

His mind was racing, trying to figure out what happened last night, but his head was all fuzzy from the medication. He just couldn't think straight.

He wobbled into the kitchen and made a pot of coffee. After pouring himself a mugful of the steaming brew, he sat down at the kitchen table.

There was a brand new Bible sitting there with a red book marker sticking out, so he opened it and began to read an underlined scripture.

"Humble yourselves therefore under the mighty hand of God, that he may exalt you in due time. Casting all your care upon Him; for he careth for you. Be sober, be vigilant; because

your adversary the devil, as a roaring lion, walketh about seeking whom he may devour."

"Amen to that," he said, and then it struck him. "Wait a minute," he said, and he re-read the letter from the church. "Dammit! Daddy *was* here! This Bible was supposed to be on the nightstand! Oh, Lord, have mercy!" he cried.

After two more mugs of coffee, and making certain all the doors and windows were locked, Chester took a shower and then went back to sleep, this time minus the sleeping pills.

When he woke up, it was nearly four in the afternoon. He dragged himself into the living room and turned on the small TV the church had graciously left for him. Margot Smith was on and Chester thought about Wanda Faye and his children. Then, he thought about the strange and evil visitor who came in the night.

"Was it really Daddy, or did I do this to myself?" he wondered, not quite sure about anything anymore.

He so wished he could go to Wanda Faye and beg her forgiveness for the wrongs he had inflicted upon her. He knew full well now the pain suffered by those who are systematically abused.

He had known it as a child standing in the tubs of scalding water, and he inflicted it on Wanda Faye as a young adult, thinking it was a way of expressing his care and love. He endured it at the hands of Daddy and found that love was not even one small part of the equation of the abuse cycle. Power was the primary aphrodisiac of abuse.

He knew now that true love, the love Jesus spoke about, the love you were supposed to express and feel for someone, had nothing to do with power, jealousy or feeling you must have the upper hand. Love was unselfish, unending and unconditional.

It had taken three years of abuse at Daddy's hands and months of therapy in prison before he came to that conclusion. The visitor in the night scared him to death. He was still frightened, but more than his fear of dying, Chester realized he felt much lighter and much better now than he did yesterday. He decided to write down a master goal on a sheet of paper.

"Put the past in the past and leave it there," he wrote, and then he turned his attention back to Margot.

"We've all made mistakes in our lives," she said. "I've made them. Every one of us have. If we learn from those mistakes and try to make our lives better, fuller and richer, in spite of our mistakes, then we are accomplishing something major in our lives."

"Amen to that," Chester said.

Chapter 25

The House of Prayer was full to overflowing on the Sunday evening Miss Jewell and Sister Velma returned from their trip to the Holy Land. Everyone in the congregation was anxious to see their slide presentation of pictures and hear about their experiences.

Sister Velma was operating the slide projector, while Miss Jewell did the majority of the talking. As she told them of their trip to the Wailing Wall, where she and Sister Velma prayed and spent time giving out pamphlets printed with the Plan of Salvation, she spoke about the friendliness of the people and being able to feel the presence of the Holy Ghost.

When Sister Velma clicked to the slide of the two of them being baptized in the River Jordan by Brother Lenny Lister, Miss Jewell seemed overcome with emotion.

"I'm sorry," Miss Jewell said. "Give me a moment," she added, as she choked back tears and dabbed at her eyes with a tissue.

Sister Velma moved on to the next few slides that showed more of their baptismal experience in the river, while Miss Jewell tried to compose herself.

Sister Mary Lee was at the piano and she broke into a hymn called, "Shall We Gather at the River", followed by another hymn, "At the Crossing of the Jordan".

At the end of the presentation, everyone in the church commented on how wonderful and inspirational it was, and they thanked Miss Jewell and Sister Velma for sharing their uplifting experiences with them.

Right before the service ended, Miss Jewell and Sister Velma presented Sister Mary Lee with a beautiful gold necklace. Hanging from it was a cross that had been carved from olive wood. Sister Mary Lee was beside herself as she accepted the gift, and then she hugged both women.

"I shall wear this to church every Sunday," she said, as she clutched it to her bosom.

Miss Jewell and Sister Velma then publicly thanked Nadine and Wanda Faye for the opportunity of a lifetime they had been privileged to experience. They also thanked Destini for making all the arrangements for their trip.

At the reception following the evening worship service, Miss Jewell couldn't stop talking about two wonderful women, sisters in Christ, she said, whom they met on their trip, by the names of Eloise Green and Martha White.

"They're from Geneva, Alabama," Miss Jewell said. "These two ladies are very involved in their church, and they told us they raised a lot of money by baking cakes and selling them to folks in their community. Miss Martha said they made over ten-thousand dollars last year just selling all those cakes."

"Well, Mama, nobody can bake a chocolate swirl cake like you can," Wanda Faye piped up. "Folks are always asking how you get that swirl so perfectly centered in the middle of the cake."

"You make delicious sour cream pound cakes and red velvet cakes, too, Mama," Nadine chimed in.

"If you ask me, there's nobody who can make a better old fashioned coconut cake with that seven-minute icing than Sister Velma," Miss Jewell said. "Oh, and her famous multi-layered chocolate cake with boiled icing is just fabulous," she added, licking her lips.

After more conversation about cakes and who could make the best kinds, all the ladies came up with an idea they hoped would benefit the entire congregation. Since the church was equipped with an up-to-date, modern kitchen, complete with two new heavy duty mixers, the ladies decided to start their own cake baking business and see where it would lead them.

As they talked about this new endeavor, Nadine rolled her eyes at Wanda Faye.

"A darn trip of a lifetime to the Holy Land, and all Mama can talk about is being the new Pentecostal Betty Crocker," Nadine whispered to Wanda Faye, and the two girls shared a private laugh together.

"Well, since there's no stoppin' her now, how about you and me and Destini go up to Sam's Club in Valdosta tomorrow and stock up on supplies like extract, sugar, cake flour and butter," Wanda Faye suggested.

"Are you crazy?" Nadine gasped. "Look what we've already spent on them!"

"Think about it this way," Destini said, stepping between the two girls. "Y'all got a weddin', huntin' season's about to start, Thanksgivin's just around the corner, and Christmas is comin' up real quick. How do y'all wanna handle all that? You want Miss Jewell on top of y'all every single day, aggravatin' the horns off a bull? Or, would you rather have her busy doin' the work of the Lord and makin' these cakes to sell?"

Nadine looked over at Wanda Faye, and seconds later, she said, "Get a pen and a piece of paper, Destini. Let's start writin' that list."

All the girls had a good laugh.

"While we're at it, let's get Mr. Hamp to place the first big order for the Camp. You call him tonight, Destini," Nadine said.

"No need to call, girl," Destini said. "I'm the

one in charge of gettin' the groceries for the lodge. We'll start out with a dozen cake mixes for each kind these ladies bake. That should keep 'em busy till more orders start rollin' in."

As Wanda Faye sipped on her punch, she thought, "God works in mysterious ways, his wonders to perform."

"You know, God parted the Red Sea for the Hebrew children to cross over on dry land and escape Pharaoh's army," Wanda Faye told the girls. "Then, he put Mama in touch with the cake baking ladies from Alabama and gave her a new purpose in life to keep her out of my hair a while," she added.

As the girls shared another private laugh together, Wanda Faye thought to herself, "Thank you, Lord."

Chapter 26

Even in the midst of all the wedding preparations for Wanda Faye and Dink's upcoming nuptials, there was still plenty of time reserved for leisurely talking, a little bit of fun, and hours of simple relaxation. There was even time for some startling revelations.

It was on a beautiful fall afternoon at Camp EZ that Wanda Faye, Nadine and Destini were lounging on the front porch, enjoying a pot of coffee Destini had made from a divine Jamaican blend that was given to her by one of the hunting guests at the lodge.

Along with the coffee, they were savoring samples of some of the Salvation Sweets cakes that Miss Jewell had brought home yesterday. Salvation Sweets was the name the church ladies had given to their new cake baking business.

"This multi-layered chocolate cake with fudge icing is the best, isn't it?" Nadine asked the other two girls.

"I like 'em all," Destini said, as she slid another forkful of coconut cake between her lips.

Soon, they were arguing back and forth about which cake should be served as dessert for the rehearsal dinner. Destini kept insisting the old fashioned coconut cake with the seven minute icing was her top pick.

"Here's an idea," Nadine said. "Why don't we offer both of them and see which one gets devoured first. Then, we'll know which one is the best for Wanda Faye's wedding cake."

"Sorry, girls, I want the lemon pound cake, decorated with white butter cream icing, and an arrangement of pink roses and baby's breath as the top layer," Wanda Faye told them.

She also told them the groom's cake would have to be her mama's chocolate swirl cake, since it was Dink's favorite.

"Then, we can set out other selections from Salvation Sweets on another table," Wanda Faye added.

Destini laughed, and said, "Just make sure to have plenty of that coconut, girl. You know me and Bunnye, Duke, Essie, and Mama Tee all love that cake. 'Course knowin' Mama Tee, she's goin' make me give her plenty of insulin, so she can have a taste of all of 'em. Knowin' your mama, she'll wait on Mama Tee like a queen and bring her some of all them cakes."

All the girls had a good laugh, and then, out of the blue, the conversation turned to the subject of school and the recent controversy that had the community up in arms. It all started a couple months ago when a letter was sent home with the students for their parents to read.

There was a separate attachment to the letter that was titled, "Types of Families". It stated that a family could be traditional or non-traditional, and that it was within the definition of the non-traditional family where problems arose.

The information was research-based and up-to-date, according to Superintendent Homer Janaydus Jenkins Jr., who was better known as Stump or Stumpy Jenkins by most folks in the county. He was given that moniker because of his diminutive stature and the fact he wore small, black Santa Claus type boots with all of his ill-fitting suits.

In the letter, there was a section describing the family as being a mother only, a father only, a father and another man, a mother and another woman, grandparents as guardians, and the foster family.

This unit of study was being mandated in all the county schools from kindergarten through sixth grade, and it affected all the girls' children. It was part of the physical education curriculum centered on the family they were told.

The subject had proven to be more controversial than the superintendent and the school board could have imagined at their last few meetings.

Brother Linton and members of the local clergy were outraged about the program, so Stumpy Jenkins eventually offered a mild concession, which the school board narrowly approved by a vote of three to two. It was agreed that parts of the curriculum about non-traditional families would not be over-emphasized. It pacified, but in no way satisfied the majority of the parents in attendance at last night's school board meeting, which all three girls had attended.

"Destini, does Bunnye ever ask you anything about her daddy?" Wanda Faye asked.

"Never mentions it," Destini said. "I guess her life's so full with y'all and your children, she ain't had time to think about it. One time, all on her own, she told me she had so many mamas and daddies who loved her, including y'all, your mama, Uncle Louie, Mama Tee, Uncle Duke, Aunt Essie and Miss Jewell. She said she was a lucky girl."

Wanda Faye and Nadine were both brought to tears by Destini's words, and there were hugs all around.

The conversation took yet another turn, as Destini recounted a story she told the girls about visiting Duke and Essie in Gainesville nearly six years ago. She obviously didn't recall having told them before, which could have been because she was drunk as a skunk the first time she told them.

She said she had gone to a party with Essie's niece, Tanzie. While there, someone put something in her drink. She said she drank a few sips and then couldn't remember anything after that, other than she woke up hours later in an abandoned house and discovered her underclothes had been torn off. There was semen on the dirty, old mattress, she said, and dried semen between her thighs and legs.

"It was a horrific experience," Destini said.

As she listened to the story a second time, Wanda Faye felt extreme sorrow for her, as she could well relate to the experience. Other than the first time Destini had told them the story, there had never been any mention of it until now.

Wanda Faye and Nadine often talked about it in private, though, and they both had a lot of unanswered questions, as well as a few suspicions.

Throughout her pregnancy with Bunnye, Destini went to the best OB/GYN doctor in Gainesville, had the best pre-natal care money could buy, and delivered Bunnye at the Women's Center, a private hospital. When questioned about it right before the birth, Destini told the girls that Duke and Essie had paid for everything, and the girls accepted her explanation, until she brought the baby back home to Seraph Springs.

Bunnye, it turned out, had an extremely light

skin tone. It was odd because Destini was dark as dark could be, as were her relatives. They weren't what most people would refer to as coal shuttle black, but they were certainly not bright skinned, as folks used to say in the Deep South.

Destini, as well as the rest of her living relatives, had eyes the color of polished chocolate. Bunnye, on the other hand, had bright blue eyes.

Destini claimed Bunnye took after Mama Tee's mother, who had blue eyes, a thin, perky nose, and thin, straight lips, as her daddy was Dee Dee Wilson's great-grandfather.

Born and raised in north Florida, Wanda Faye and Nadine both knew a thing or two about skin tone among blacks. They knew the difference between a bright skinned black, one who may have had a white or Indian great-grandfather, and mulattos, who had blue, green or grayish eyes. It usually suggested a white man was the father of the baby. Wanda Faye, for one, was certain Bunnye's father had to have been a white man... an unknown white man at a party, who raped their precious Destini.

Ever since Bunnye was born, Destini stopped dating men... period. She seemed to have no interest in hooking up with anyone. She joked about them on occasion, like the time she told the girls to bring Denzel Washington home for her, but other than that, she didn't date or go out to clubs.

Her life revolved around Bunnye, Mama Tee, her church, her job at Camp EZ, and hanging out with the girls. She seemed happy enough and perfectly content, but oftentimes, Wanda Faye wondered if there was something else going on.

As they finished up the last of the coffee, Nadine and Wanda Faye both lit up a cigarette.

"There's one thing I'm goin' tell you girls," Destini said. "We ain't gonna be smokin' no nasty cigarettes the day of the weddin'. Y'all better make arrangements, cause they ain't gonna be no white trashy lookin' pictures with y'all havin' them cigarettes dangling out the sides of y'alls mouths. Y'all ought to try and quit them nasty things. They done shot up to nearly six bucks a pack, and you got some beautiful children and everything in the world to live for."

Wanda Faye and Nadine looked at one another and they both just shrugged their shoulders in defeat.

"Oh, all right," Nadine said. "No smoking during the weddin'. I ain't promising about the rest of the day just yet."

Destini's demeanor seemed to drastically change all of a sudden. She looked nervous and started fidgeting with her clothes, as if there was more on her mind than just cigarettes.

"Destini, what's wrong?" Wanda Faye asked. "You look like you just seen a ghost or somethin'."

Destini sat up straight in her chair and sucked in a huge breath.

"Well," she started, diverting her eyes, as if what she was about to say was the most embarrassing thing in the world. "It's about that midnight train to Ludowici," she said, and then she looked straight into Wanda Faye's eyes.

"Oh, that's right," Nadine said. "You ain't told us a thing about that night. What was it all about? And for godsakes, what happened?"

Destini shrugged, and looked as if she changed her mind about telling them.

"Come on, girl," Wanda Faye said. "Whatever it is, you know you can trust us."

"Well, they's not a whole helluva lot to tell," she said. "As Mr. Hamp often says, I went, I saw, I conquered."

"Conquered what?" Wanda Faye asked.

"Well, y'all ain't gonna be worried about no Chester Easley comin' down here, or writing no more letters, but I gotta tell both y'all, that man didn't look none too good to me."

"You saw him?" Wanda Faye gasped.

"Yes'm, I sho' did. I seen pictures you have of him with you and the children, Miss Wanda Faye, and what I saw up there in Ludowici was not the same man. Hair's all gray, deep lines around his eyes that were all sunk back in his head."

"You saw him up in Ludowici?" Wanda Faye asked, still in shock.

"I paid him a visit," Destini bluntly said, and then she related the entire story to the girls, from the time she bought the straight razor, to the late hour she broke into Chester's grandma's house, to the time she walked out the door, feeling satisfied she had scared the living daylights out of him.

"Lord, he didn't look nothin' like the angry man in them letters after I got through with him," Destini said. "More like a scared baby. 'Course, I did have that blade down there on his business. As I was goin' out that door, that man said somethin' to me that put the chills all over me."

"What did he say?" Nadine asked.

"He said for me to tell Wanda Faye that he knew how she felt 'cause he felt the same way now. Then he told me I was the Lord's messenger... an angel sent from the Lord hisself."

"You reckon he lost his mind in jail?" Wanda Faye asked her.

"I dunno, Miss Wanda Faye. All I knows is he was real calm when he said it to me, and it put the chills all over my body, the same way as when the preacher and all them folks start prayin' and screamin', and talkin' in tongues. It was that kind of feelin'."

"I still say the man is crazy as a bedbug," Nadine said, shaking her head. "And so are you for goin' up there to see him."

"Well, I don't know 'bout that," Destini said with a chuckle. "The Lord can do anythin', you know. If he can send an angel to earth ridin' on a fiery lookin' horse and carryin' a sword, then he can sho' send a woman in a beat up, old pickup to Georgia with a three-hundred dollar switch blade."

Even though Wanda Faye was stunned beyond belief at Destini's confession, deep in her heart she felt a sense of peace that Chester would not be bothering her ever again.

"The two of you better remember when y'all around me from now on that I'm an angel," Destini said, trying to inject some humor into the situation. "Yep, y'all better mind my wings and tell me if my halo starts gettin' a little rusty or tarnished."

With that statement, all the girls roared with laughter, until tears ran down their faces.

Wanda Faye thought about the many blessings in her life, as she laughed with Nadine and Destini. Then, she thought about Miss Margot and visualized something she might have said on her TV program, although, she'd never heard her say it.

"True friends are those who know you and love you anyway. Yes, ma'am," Wanda Faye thought. "That is what love is."

Chapter 27

Wanda Faye and Dink's wedding preparations were moving along perfectly, with one small exception. On a Saturday morning, a few days before the wedding, Wanda Faye went up to Miss Sissy's shop to speak to her one last time about doing the hair for all the members of the wedding party.

While she was there, Miss Sissy asked her to go out to her car and bring in the hairstyle magazines she had stacked on the backseat. She said she had marked the ones she thought were wonderful and elegant updo's.

As Wanda Faye was rummaging through the backseat of Miss Sissy's Cadillac, something poked her underneath one of her fingernails.

"Ow!" she whimpered.

Whatever it was that poked her seemed to be wedged between the bench seat and the upright. When she lifted up a pile of magazines, she saw a square, hard plastic card and figured Miss Sissy must have misplaced one of her charge cards.

She yanked it out from the creases in the white, leather seat and when she looked at it closely, she nearly choked on her saliva.

"What the hell is Dink's driver's license doing here?" she gasped.

Dink had told her about his fling with Miss Sissy when she first came to town. It was after their pre-marital session with Brother Linton. He told her he wanted no secrets between them and felt obligated to tell her.

Wanda Faye had never mentioned it to Miss Sissy, or to anyone else, for that matter, not even Nadine or Destini. She figured, why stir up something and cause trouble for someone who had been so sweet and kind to her? Miss Sissy was human, after all, just like Dink.

Since neither of them were married at the time, Wanda Faye felt they were entitled to their little tryst, but this… this was a different matter.

She wasn't sure what to do, so for now, she just shoved it into the pocket of her blue jeans to deal with later. She went back into the shop with the magazines under her arm and told Miss Sissy she'd look at them at home and give her a call later.

As she was leaving, Miss Sissy turned to Lollie, and said, "I wonder what's wrong with her. She's running like her tail is on fire. I guess it's just nerves, God bless her. I know everything's gonna be fine. It's gonna be real nice."

As Wanda Faye drove home, her mind was all tangled, the way it had been when she got the letter from Chester. She was sure there was a reasonable explanation for Dink's license being in the back of Miss Sissy's car. There had to be.

She figured she'd just nonchalantly hand it to him and then see what he said. She didn't plan on doing this alone, though. It would require getting her sister in on the act. After all, Nadine could spot a liar at fifty paces and she'd know in an instant if Dink was lying.

Instead of going home, she swung by Nadine's place. As she pulled into the drive, she spotted her outside watering her chrysanthemums. Nadine had always loved flowers. Even when she lived in her old beat up trailer, she always kept a small flower bed filled with seasonal plants, as well as herbs and spices.

As soon as Wanda Faye stepped out of the truck, Nadine took one look at her and asked, "What's wrong? You got trouble. I can see it in your eyes."

"I just came from Miss Sissy's and when I went out to her car to get some hairstyling magazines, I found Dink's driver's license in her backseat. It wasn't no old license, neither, Nadine. It's his current one."

Wanda Faye felt she had no choice now but to tell Nadine about Dink and Miss Sissy's past fling, and so she did in fifty words or less.

"Well, he's coming by here in just a little while to look at an old truck Louie has to see if they can get the thing runnin'," Nadine told her.

"Oh, no, what do I do?" Wanda Faye asked.

"Come on inside, bring the license with you, and don't act nervous. As soon as he gets here, I'll invite him and Louie to come sit down here in the kitchen for some cake and coffee. As for you, just as sweet as pie, you say to him, 'Dink, I went out to Miss Sissy's Cadillac to get some hairstyling magazines and I found your driver's license. I brought them to you, honey.' Don't ask him how it got there. Don't be confrontational. Just make those statements and then watch his reaction."

"How did you get so smart about how to deal with people, Nadine?"

"Sister, it's called experience," Nadine said, and she put her arm around Wanda Faye's shoulder. "It's about watching your back and knowing how to watch other people's backs. I learned it early on. I may not have a big college degree, and I may not have a high level job, but I got a doctorate in knowing how to watch somebody's back, and in knowing all about human nature."

"I really appreciate you helping me with this," Wanda Faye said.

"That's what I'm here for. I'll tell you something else I got. I got a built in system, like one of them metal detectors that buzzes when it gets over a piece of metal. My system don't make no sound, but when it gets around fakes and bullshitters, it dings really loud. It's like a siren in my head. Look, when you hit Dink broadside out of the blue with this, if he's lying, I'll know it."

"I hope you're right, Nadine, and I hope Dink don't try to lie," Wanda Faye said.

"Same here," Nadine said. "All right, now. You go on back to the bathroom and straighten your hair up, wash your face and put some makeup on," she ordered her. "You been crying and you don't want Dink to know you're upset."

Chapter 28

As Wanda Faye was coming out of the bathroom, she could hear Nadine rattling around in the kitchen. Then, she heard the familiar rumble of Dink's pickup pulling into the yard and going around to the back of the house where Louie was in the garage. The next thing she heard was Nadine opening the backdoor, so she slipped into her bedroom.

"Louie! Dink! Come on inside a minute!" Nadine shouted. "That means now, Louie!"

"Aw, Nadine, can't you see I'm busy?!" Louie shot back, nearly cracking his head on the hood of the truck he was working on. "Can't this wait?"

"No, it can't wait! Come on in the damned house now before I have to hurt you!"

"Hey, come on, Louie. We got plenty of time to work on this old heap," Dink said, as he joined him in the garage. "I wanna go inside anyway and say hey to Wanda Faye."

All the kids had gone to the movies over in Pittstown with Destini and Bunnye, so there would be no interruptions while Nadine and Wanda Faye attempted to get to the bottom of the situation as to how and why Dink's driver's license found its way into the backseat of Miss Sissy's car.

Louie came ambling in first with Dink right on his heels.

"I promise this won't hurt, Louie," Nadine sneered at him. "Now, go wash your hands and take those damned dirty caps off your heads," she told both of them. "How many times I gotta tell you, Louie? You don't wear caps or hats in the house."

Louie didn't say a word, but he did shoot her the bird. Luckily for him, Nadine didn't see the gesture or there would have been hell to pay. The cap came off, though, and so did Dink's. Then, the two of them went down the hall to the bathroom to wash their hands.

Meanwhile, Wanda Faye spritzed herself with some of Nadine's cologne and then hurried out to the kitchen. Minutes later, Louie and Dink came back.

"Well, hey, baby," Dink said, and he gave Wanda Faye a kiss on the cheek.

Wanda Faye noticed that Nadine had been busy in the kitchen. The table was all laid out with coffee mugs, plates, forks, spoons, napkins, cream, sugar, and artificial sweetener, along with a sample platter of Miss Jewell's cakes, sliced real thin. The aroma of percolating coffee had already filled the house with an intoxicating and inviting scent.

"Is that some of that wonderful coffee Destini gave us the other day out at the lodge?" Wanda Faye asked.

"It sure is. I liked it so much, I asked her for some," Nadine said. "Since they were in individual packets that would make a whole pot, she gave me four of them. I like my coffee a little stronger, so I used a pack and about a quarter of another one."

After everyone sat down, Nadine asked them to hold hands around the table, so she could say the blessing.

"Lord, we thank you for this time to be with our loved ones, and for the wonderful truth of love and friendship," Nadine started.

Wanda Faye cracked open her eyes and saw that Nadine was staring directly at Dink as she spoke.

"We know in your holy words you tell us the truth will set us free, and we glorify your name, knowing we have the love of those around us today," Nadine continued. "Thank you, Lord, for Salvation Sweets and these cakes, and for the cake baking business that's keepin' Mama busy and out mine and Wanda Faye's hair right now. Continue to bless them, Lord, as you have blessed our family. In the name of Jesus, we pray. Amen."

"You know, Mama wouldn't have been all that proud of that prayer, Nadine, but, I gotta hand it to you, it was honest," Wanda Faye said, grinning. "I'm thankful Mama met them women from Alabama. Since she had them cards printed up and distributed around town, she's had about twenty-five or thirty orders for cakes already. Her phone's been ringing off the hook with folks asking her about the holidays."

"That's good," Nadine said. "Mama's always happiest when she's busy. These cakes, along with her Bible Drill will keep her moving on the Jericho Road. It won't be long before she'll have that Bible Drill team in the kitchen with her cleaning up mixing bowls, breaking eggs and measuring ingredients for her, as they memorize them Bible verses."

"Yep, Mama will figure a way to make it all work for her," Wanda Faye said. "I have no doubts."

Once everyone started eating, Nadine looked over at Wanda Faye and winked at her.

"So, did you find any hairstyles in Miss Sissy's magazines that you thought would be good for you and me?" Nadine asked her. "You know, somethin' to make us look like glamorous movie stars. I'll betcha by the time Miss Sissy gets through with us, Louie and Dink will be so hot for us, we might not be able to make it through the weddin'. Ain't that right, Louie, honey?"

Nadine reached over and rumpled Louie's hair and then kissed him on the cheek.

"Stop that, Nadine," he said, pushing her hand away. "Don't mess with my beautiful coiffure. It took me thirty long seconds to get it just right this morning with the wash cloth... all four strands of it."

Everyone had a good laugh and then Wanda Faye, as cool as a cucumber, turned toward Dink and smiled as innocently as she could. Then she slid his driver's license across the table to him.

"Honey, I found this under some magazines in the backseat of Miss Sissy's car this morning," she said. "I figured you'd be needin' it."

"Oh, thanks, Wanda Faye," he said, without a trace of nervousness in his voice. "I been lookin' for that."

"Is that it?" Nadine asked, looking him straight in the eyes.

Dink's face turned red and then he cleared his throat and turned to Wanda Faye.

"I was hopin' to keep this as a surprise for you, Wanda Faye, but since the cat's out of the bag, I guess I'll have to tell you," he added, and then he shot Nadine the evil eye.

"Yes, please do," Nadine urged him.

"Nadine, this ain't what you think," he said. "I went to Miss Sissy's last week and I paid for all you girls to have your hair done... you know, as a weddin' gift. I gave them Vietnamese gals money, too, for y'all to get your nails done."

"You did?" Wanda Faye asked, seemingly already convinced he did no wrong.

"Yes, I did," Dink said. "Since Mr. Hamp wouldn't let me give him one dime for us having the rehearsal supper out there at the camp, and your mama wouldn't take no money for the cakes, and I already bought the ring... well, I figured I'd go see Miss Sissy and pay for y'all's hair appointments."

"Oh, Dink, that was so thoughtful of you," Wanda Faye said, and she leaned over and kissed him on the mouth.

"That don't explain how your driver's license wound up in her backseat," Nadine said, as she shoved a piece of cake into her mouth.

"I was gettin' to that," Dink said, sounding irritated now. "While I was at Miss Sissy's, she asked me to check the speakers in her car. She said she thought there might be a short in the wires or something."

"Yeah, go on," Nadine said.

"Well, I guess I was in a hurry when I left the house, 'cause I dropped my wallet and everything fell out all over the floor. I shoved it all back in and put my wallet in my back pocket. As I was walkin' out the door, I noticed my license was still layin' on the floor, so I picked it up and stuck it in my shirt pocket. Like I said, I was in a hurry.

I guess it fell out when I was workin' on Miss Sissy's speakers."

Wanda Faye smiled and looked over at Nadine, who shrugged her shoulders, as if she believed his story.

"Well, Dink, I think you are the sweetest thing in the whole world," Wanda Faye said, and she kissed him on the cheek. "You don't need to eat any more of this cake to get no sweeter. Does he, Nadine?"

Nadine just rolled her eyes and shoved another piece of cake into her mouth.

"Well, ladies, I'd like to sit here and chit chat with y'all, but me and Dink got work to do," Louie said, wiping his mouth with a napkin as he stood up. "Come on, Dink. I think I figured out what's wrong with that old truck."

"Yeah, me and Nadine have a lot to do still to get ready for the big day, so y'all get on outta here," Wanda Faye said, anxious to be alone with her sister.

"Well, Sister Velma, Sister Mary Lee, and the Bible Drill team have taken over the preparations for the reception," Nadine said. "They're doing the refreshments, the decorations... everything. Destini, Duke and Mr. Hamp are doing most everything for the rehearsal supper, so there ain't much for us to do, except get the children dressed and ready, as well as ourselves. Louie, did you tell me you know where a couple of them electric cattle prods are?" she asked, as he and Dink were about to slip out the door. "We're gonna need 'em on the weddin' day. I can see it now, me riding roughshod on the youngun's with that prod hollering Hey-ya! Round 'em up and head em out!"

"Nadine, you ain't right," Louie said, laughing. "You ain't never been. I guess that's why we get along so well, because I sho' ain't right."

"No, you ain't," Nadine agreed. "But you ain't one hundred per cent wrong, neither. Maybe that's what I love about you," she added, and then gave him a full mouth kiss. "Now, go on and get that truck fixed. Me and Wanda Faye want y'all to drive us out to the camp when you get it fired up. We gotta see Destini about a couple things. Y'all can drive us out there like we're on a double date. Just like old times, eh, Louie?"

Louie just shook his head and hurried out the door with Dink trailing behind him. Once they were far enough away, Wanda Faye let loose.

"Well? What do you think? What do you think, sis?"

"I think Dink knows how to think real fast on his feet," she said. "That's what I think."

"Oh, come on, Nadine. You're making way too much out of this."

"Sweetie, I don't doubt he paid for the hair appointments, and I don't doubt Miss Sissy wanted him to look at something in that Cadillac.

What I *do* doubt is what *she* wanted to look at when he got out there. I ain't buyin' all that crap about the license in the front pocket thing. No ma'am, and I'll tell you, Wanda Faye, as nice as she's been, I'm thinking when this weddin' is over, we might need to find somebody else to style our hair."

"Oh, come on," Wanda Faye said. "You can't be serious."

"I'm dead serious! Since we go to Pittstown a lot more than Turpricone, we can just tell her with the children and all, it's more convenient for us. Then, if Dink ever heads up in that direction, trust me, your sister will know. I got a good friend who works across the street from her shop as manager of the dollar store and she'll be more than happy to be on the lookout for me. She's got eyes like an eagle."

"I think Louie has you pegged," Wanda Faye said. "You ain't right."

"Look, Wanda Faye. If somethin' happened between Dink and Miss Sissy, we'll just let it go for the time being. No need stirrin' you know what up right now with the weddin' comin' up and all, but as Mama often quotes from the scripture, and I ain't quoting it just right, but, "as a dog returns to his vomit, so a fool returns to his folly."

Wanda Faye didn't know what to think anymore, but for the time being, she truly believed

Dink was telling the truth.

"You done good today, sis," Nadine said. "Matlock couldn't have been more cool than you was when you brought that license out. I was proud of you. Just keep on being cool. Dink's a good man and you're a young woman, and Miss Sissy's old. She's got charm, honey, but she's old."

"Oh, she's not that old."

"Trust me, she's old," Nadine said. "Dink may have something between his legs that she wants from time to time, though. From what you told me, he's got somethin' most any woman would want, but you're the one he chose to marry, not her."

"I know that," Wanda Faye said.

"She put him down years ago for money. You might want to remind him of that later on. Take it from me, I know you ain't as aggressive as I am, but if you wanna keep that man at home, you need to be the hunter once in a while. Men love it when they think a woman wants 'em. It does wonders for their male ego, and that's somethin' us women gotta stroke more than they do. It usually goes hand in hand, no pun intended."

Wanda Faye couldn't help but laugh.

"Miss Sissy's a smart one and she's foxy, but she ain't hunted in these woods as long as I have. I know all the secret holes and hidin' places around here, and how to watch and not get caught. If Miss Sissy's slippin' and slidin' with Dink, I'll find it out, and it won't take me that long. In the meantime, you just keep on with your plans and keep a smile on that pretty face. Dink is yours, and he's gonna stay yours. Don't forget that."

Wanda Faye smiled, but deep inside she felt the pangs of that old ache she had the day she and Dink prayed with Brother Linton. She wondered if this gnawing pain at the core of her heart would ever go away.

She wished she could pick up the phone and speak to Miss Margot. She was certain she'd have words of wisdom for her. Right now, though, she had to move on, and she had to think only the best about Dink and trust him.

Chapter 29

On the afternoon of the wedding rehearsal, the air was crisp and cool, and the skies were clear and filled with golden sunshine. Inside the House of Prayer everything was polished and shined, and glistened like fine china.

Brother Linton took the helm and complimented everyone for making the sanctuary look so beautiful. He recognized Hattie Wilson Campbell, her sister, Miss Nanny, and their niece Dee Dee, stating they had put together some of the most stunning spring floral decorations, despite the fact it was the middle of autumn.

The women had inserted asparagus fern and variegated ivy, which they got from Mrs. Frank's garden, into the flower arrangements. Dee Dee had told Wanda Faye they would wait until tomorrow to place the pink and yellow spray roses, and the white daisies into each arrangement.

The ribbons used in the arrangements were selected by Essie and Destini. They matched the dotted Swiss floral background fabric that was part of the bridal attendants' dresses. The same ribbon also cascaded down the sides of the pews in bright, vivid colors. Since it was going to be a morning wedding there was no need for candles.

Immediately following the rehearsal, which went off without a hitch, the entire wedding party, including Brother Linton and Sister Velma, Jerri Faye, Miss Hattie, Miss Nanny, and Dee Dee, went out to Camp EZ for the rehearsal dinner.

"Have you ever seen such a spread?" Wanda Faye said in awe after she and Dink went out on the back screened porch where they would be having dinner.

"Yeah, it's darned nice," Dink said.

There were five large, round tables that seated twelve people each, and every table had a birds-eye view of the majestic, slow moving, dark waters of the Suwannee River. Its high banks were dotted with tupelo, cypress and saw palmettos. The scene was beyond enchanting and so fitting for the special occasion.

Wanda Faye loved palmetto fans, so Miss Hattie had placed a huge arrangement of them, along with pine cone lilies, pyracantha and nandina on the buffet tables. Hurricane lamps with bayberry candles served as the centerpieces for the dining tables, and they emanated an intoxicating fragrance throughout the patio area.

Since it was the fall of the year and the rehearsal dinner was at the hunting lodge, Wanda Faye agreed to allow Miss Hattie to use seasonal arrangements. The masculine décor of Camp EZ simply wasn't conducive to using pastels, Miss Hattie told her.

The buffet table seemed to be groaning under the weight of all the food. Mr. Hamp, Duke, Essie, and Destini had outdone themselves. There was barbecued venison, beef, pork and chicken, as well as baked beans, potato salad, a relish tray full of homemade pickles and preserves, a huge pot of chicken pilau, collards and turnip greens, and tiny acre peas and fall peas from Miss Hattie's and Miss Nanny's farms.

On each table were buttermilk biscuits and cornbread that were covered with cloth and steaming in their baskets. Of course, no dinner in this region of north Florida would be complete without deviled eggs, and Destini made the best in the world. There was a platter of them on each table.

On the dessert table were Miss Jewell's cakes and a variety of her pies, including pecan, sweet potato and chess. There was also plenty of sweet tea, water and steaming hot coffee.

Once everyone figured out where they were supposed to sit, Brother Linton said the blessing. Then, Wanda Faye and Dink led the group through the buffet line.

No sooner had Wanda Faye put her plate down than she was back in line trying to help her children fill their plates.

"Honey, you go sit down," Destini told her. "Sit down and eat, girl. We'll take care of these children. Go on, now. Go on and sit down with your fiancé."

The evening couldn't have been more perfect or more memorable, Wanda Faye thought, as she gazed into the eyes of the man she was about to marry. The food was divine, the company was exceptional, and everyone seemed to be thoroughly enjoying themselves.

When Mr. Hamp gave the couple a brand new freezer chest full of beef, pork and venison, Wanda Faye broke down in tears. There was an audible gasp from the small crowd when Miss Hattie and Miss Nanny gave the couple an invitation for a holiday reception to be given in their honor the Saturday before Christmas at the historic Campbell home in Turpricone.

The two women had been hosting their Christmas party for over fifty years, and never once in all those years had they thrown it in honor of anyone. Miss Hattie, in her simple, rust-colored, silk pantsuit told Wanda Faye and Dink how special they were to her and to everyone.

"Y'all are the only couple I've ever honored at my holiday reception, but this year I am proud to do it for you," she told them. "Dink, I couldn't have kept my mowing and lawn equipment going through the years if it hadn't been for you. You've never turned me down, and I know I'm an old woman and aggravating as hell."

Everyone laughed, albeit quietly, and then Miss Hattie continued.

"Wanda Faye, you'll make a good nurse. I hope you'll be as good a one as your mama and Sister Velma. Don't think I've forgotten the time Dee Dee was so sick with that fever and flu. Your mama and Sister Velma came to the house and never left that child's side or mine. I've never been an over-emotional woman, but I want you both to know I love you, and so do Nanny and Dee Dee. The fact this old fool, my childhood friend, Hamp Brayerford, would spend this kind of money on you, must tell you something. Heck, since my husband died, all I've been trying to get out of him is a solitaire diamond. Not a small one, Hamp, a big one!" she shouted, as she glanced over at him.

That comment sent everyone into peals of laughter, including Mr. Hamp. It seemed everyone knew Miss Hattie had a thing for him, but they were far, far away from ever tying the knot. Miss Hattie could tell a joke, though, and she did it with such finesse.

"Now, that's class," Nadine whispered to Wanda Faye.

"Yeah, but I'm sure she's wantin' somethin'

from either Dink or me, or even from Mr. Hamp."

"What do mean?"

"She's just like Miss Sissy," Wanda Faye said. "She wants somethin'. You think I ain't had her figured out all along? She don't care about you, me, or nobody else. She just wanted our money, and she got a good bit of it, but she had to do our long hair and it took some effort on her part, if you hadn't noticed. I don't want to think about that tonight, though."

"Yeah, me neither," Nadine said.

"Tomorrow, when she comes and does the comb-out for us at the church, it'll be the last we have to see of her for a long time."

"I agree," Nadine said. "Tonight, it's just eat, drink and be merry, and try to get a good night's rest for tomorrow. That reminds me, Duke and Essie's taking all the youngun's to their house to look after them tonight. Then, it's just you, me, Destini and Dee Dee who's gonna spend the night here at Camp EZ. Soon as everybody leaves, we're gonna make us some of them big coffee drinks with Bailey's Irish Cream. Then, we're gonna smoke us some cigarettes and thank the Lord for a blessed day."

"Oh, that sounds like such fun," Wanda Faye said. "I can't wait."

"I done told Louie and Dink already not to get too wasted over at Miss Evie's Bar across the river. Some of them boys they grew up with are givin' Dink a little blowout later, but they'll make it home. Hell, Sheriff Lewis is goin' out there, too, and he'll see to it they get home safe and sound."

Wanda Faye smiled at Nadine, took her by the hand, and said, "I love you. You don't know just how much I love you."

Nadine rolled her eyes, and then looked over at Destini who was sitting on the other side of her taking everything in.

"She loves me, Destini," Nadine said with a grin. "She's been the queen of this party tonight and she'll be the queen tomorrow, but me and you is gonna be first in line for them Bailey's and whipped crème tonight."

Destini chuckled and shook her head.

"The two o' you sho' is crazy," Destini said. "I guess that makes me crazy, too. I sho' is glad we ain't sane. If we was, we'd be in a heap o' trouble, wouldn't we?"

Later that night, after everyone left the lodge, the four girls enjoyed their coffee and Bailey's, and Nadine and Wanda Faye smoked one cigarette after another out on the back porch. Destini put on a Willie Nelson CD and cranked up the volume on the stereo. Appropriate as it could be, the very first song on the album was Willie singing, "I've Always Been Crazy".

Chapter 30

The next morning, everyone was at the House of Prayer early for photographs. By nine-thirty, the entire wedding party was coiffed, combed, turned out, and as many of the old folks would say, dressed to the nines.

Wanda Faye was wearing the same wedding suit worn by her mama when she and Mr. Lucius Lee married over forty years ago, right here in the same sanctuary.

Essie had taken the old cream-colored, silk suit and altered it to fit Wanda Faye and it looked fabulous on her. Even the dainty, matching hat worn by Miss Jewell all those years ago was now atop Wanda Faye's elegant coiffure. Essie had also bought her a pair of gloves that looked much like the ones her mother had worn.

Before the ceremony began, Dink surprised Wanda Faye by giving her a strand of pearls and matching pearl earrings. Since they were going to use the eternity ring he had given her when he proposed as a wedding band, he had asked Dee

Dee to help him find something special for a wedding gift for his bride. He gave her a price range of what he could afford, since he knew Dee Dee could go to the moon and back if she weren't limited.

Dee Dee found the pearls and the earrings at a small jewelry store in Jacksonville's historic Avondale section that specialized in estate jewelry. The price was right, and after talking to her Aunt Hattie, they secretly put in another five-hundred dollars as their wedding gift to the couple to purchase the jewelry. Dink had no idea.

Dee Dee helped Wanda Faye put on the necklace and earrings, and she took a step back to admire her.

"I have never seen you look more radiant than you do right now," Dee Dee told her.

Meanwhile, Charlene, Darlene, Jewell Lee and Bunnye were all dressed in tea length dresses in various shades of pastel dotted Swiss, and each of them had pastel daisies and baby's breath in their hair.

Destini and Nadine, who were serving as Maid and Matron of Honor, were wearing silk suits in pastel shades. Nadine's was a pale shade of pink and Destini's was lilac.

All the girls in the wedding party carried nosegays of pastel-colored daisies, pale pink and yellow roses, and baby's breath. Destini and Nadine carried arm bouquets. Destini's were calla lilies and irises, and Nadine's were calla lilies and long-stemmed, pale pink roses.

The blushing bride, Wanda Faye, carried her mama's little, white Bible. On top of it was a large white orchid with tiny, pale pink rosebuds and a spattering of lilies of the valley.

Dink, Louie, and all the boys looked as handsome as the setting sun on a cloudless night, dressed in blue blazers, grey flannel slacks, shiny black shoes, pastel shirts and ivory silk ties that Dee Dee had found for them in Jacksonville. Topping off their ensembles were boutonnières of ivory roses.

While Dink and Wanda Faye knelt down at the altar, Dee Dee sang an emotionally moving version of "The Lord's Prayer". There wasn't a dry eye in the house throughout the entire song.

Miss Jewell, in her pale pink suit overlaid with lace, and a beautiful orchid corsage, shouted, "Amen" when Dee Dee finished singing. It was loud enough that the entire congregation heard her.

"Thank you, sweet angel," she said to Dee Dee. "I love you."

Dee Dee never missed a beat. She was every inch a lady. Rather than be embarrassed, she blew a kiss to her old friend, and mouthed, "I love you, too."

As the soon-to-be wedded couple spoke their vows before an altar of greenery and flowers, even the children became emotional. Sister Velma fetched a tissue box and brought it up to the twins, Charlene and Darlene, who had tears streaming down their cheeks.

After the “I do’s” and the long, drawn out kiss that Dink planted on the lips of his new wife, the bride and groom marched arm in arm down the aisle of the church, followed by the entire wedding party.

Sister Mary Lee began playing an upbeat version of “Way Down Upon the Suwannee River”, while the crowd was exiting the sanctuary. Just about everyone sang along with the words they’d known by heart since they were old enough to speak.

It was truly the most memorable and special wedding the church had ever experienced. For Wanda Faye, it was as if the entire world was sharing in the love that she felt for Dink.

Chapter 31

The reception proved to be more fun than anyone could have imagined it would be. The fellowship hall looked nearly as beautiful as the sanctuary. It had been decorated by Miss Jewell's Bible Drill students and it was a sight to behold.

Big pastel wedding bells hung from the center of the ceiling, which was completely draped from one end to the other with pastel-colored crepe paper. Large balloon bouquets graced each corner of the room and the children had made a huge banner on which was written, "Congratulations Dink and Wanda Faye". Beneath it was their wedding date, and it was signed with congratulatory wishes from everyone in attendance.

Dee Dee had invited a friend of hers, who played piano at a lounge up in Valdosta, to do the entertainment. Soon beautiful music filled the hall. When she had mentioned to Wanda Faye a few weeks back about having her friend play, Wanda Faye told her it was all right as long as her mama and the preacher and his wife didn't get wind of the fact he played in a nightclub. Dee Dee assured her he was an excellent pianist and even played for the choir at his church every Sunday.

"He doesn't drink a drop," Dee Dee had told her. "He just loves to play."

Wanda Faye warned Dee Dee not to tell her mama too much about how well the guy played, or else she'd aggravate him to death about playing for revival meetings or one of her Bible Drill gatherings.

"Just say he's a good friend of yours and leave it at that," Wanda Faye had told her.

Compared to the rehearsal dinner, the refreshments for the reception were quite simple. Aside from the wedding cake and groom's cake, there was a selection of fresh fruits, cheese straws, salted and candied pecans, individual quiches, tiny pecan tartlets, bacon-wrapped dates, punch, coffee and iced tea.

What amused everyone the most was the collage the children had put together on two large bulletin boards by the door of the fellowship hall.

One contained numerous photos of Wanda Faye, Nadine and Destini, from the time they were babies up through their teen years, and then photos of them as adults with their children. There were also photos of Mama Tee, Miss Jewell, Brother Linton and Sister Velma, Jerri Faye,

Mr. Hamp, Dee Dee, and Duke and Essie.

Dink's bulletin board contained pictures of him as a baby, a young boy, and a stunningly handsome teenager, as well as more recent photos. There were ones of him with Mr. Hamp out at Camp EZ, others of him and Louie, and a few more with all his hunting and fishing buddies. There was even a photo of Dink dressed up like a pirate, which was taken on a cruise he and some of his friends went on several years ago.

All the guests spent a lot of time hovering around the two bulletin boards, laughing and joking about all the pictures.

Above every other voice in the room, was the high, shrill voice of Miss Sissy. She was over in a back corner of the hall at the moment, talking with Hattie and Nanny.

"Ain't this just so sweet and nice?" Miss Sissy squealed. "Such a sweet couple. I wish them so much happiness."

Nadine was chatting with Wanda Faye and Destini on the other side of the hall by the food tables.

"I'll be right back," Nadine said. "There's somethin' I gotta take care of," she added, and off she went.

Chapter 32

Nadine strikes again

Nadine evidently couldn't turn down the opportunity to rub a little salt into Miss Sissy's wound, so to speak, so she nonchalantly walked over toward where she was standing with Hattie and Nanny.

"That's mighty sweet of you, Miss Sissy, what you said about Wanda Faye and Dink," Nadine said. "I'll pass it on to them."

"Oh, please do," Miss Sissy said, grinning from ear to ear.

"Our hair sure does look nice, and we thank you for them pretty magazines and catalogues you sent for us to look at hairstyles."

"Oh, it was my pleasure," Miss Sissy said.

"It sure was a lucky thing that Wanda Faye found Dink's driver's license in your car. Bless his heart. He needs that license to drive for his job." Then, using one of Miss Sissy's own expressions, Nadine grinned from ear to ear, and said, "You are just the sweetest thing, Miss Sissy."

Miss Sissy's perfectly made up face immediately morphed into a blotchy mess and her cheeks turned a bright red. She set her plate and punch cup down on a nearby table and turned to the ladies she was speaking with.

"Would y'all excuse me just a second? I need to go powder my nose," she said, and she hurried off like a scared rabbit.

Nadine waited a few seconds and then she followed her into the ladies room. Miss Sissy was reapplying her makeup, and when she spotted Nadine in the mirror, she gave her a big smile.

"Well, Sunshine, there you are," she said.

"Miss Sissy, I want to talk to you about something, and I don't know quite know how to say this."

"Well, honey, just come out with it. I can assure you it ain't nothin' Miss Sissy ain't heard before."

"Well, as you know, Wanda Faye found Dink's driver's license in the backseat of your car. Dink says he just went out there to pay for our hairdos and nails, and when you asked him to check the speakers in your car, his license dropped out of his shirt pocket."

"Yes, that's right," Miss Sissy said, nodding her head.

"Well, in all the years I've known Dink, I ain't never known him to carry nothing in his front shirt pocket, except maybe an ink pen every once in a while."

"And your point is?" Miss Sissy asked, staring at her now with an evil look in her eyes.

"I know you and Dink had a little fling in the past, and I ain't judgin' you for that. What folks do before they marry is their own business, but I'm concerned about what's happening... or might be happening now, since he's involved with my sister now."

"Well, honey, you know I don't blame you a bit in the world for asking. In fact, I admire you for it. I've always believed in protecting what was mine. Two things you don't fool with around me. One is my family."

"I feel the same way," Nadine told her.

"I don't want, and I won't have people talking about my family or fooling with a member of my family, and me find out about it. In that way, me and you are a lot alike."

"Okay," Nadine said, wondering where she was going with this conversation.

"Second, is my money. I don't want folks fooling around with my money in any way, shape, form or fashion. Now, what happened here had more to do with my money, and the opportunity to make a little more. It didn't have a thing to do with Dink."

"Oh, really?"

"Really, Nadine," Miss Sissy sternly said. "I

don't mean to be hateful, honey, but I could have had Dink a long time ago, if I'd wanted him, that is. I think he's a good man, and I believe with my whole heart that he and Wanda Faye will be happy. Other than the physical side of the relationship, there wasn't a lot more between me and Dink. I always move on to where there's more of that second thing I was telling you about, money. My man now takes good care of me, and I try to take good care of him. I don't need another man. Lord, no."

Nadine was watching Miss Sissy's face the entire time she was telling her story, and she listened well. She was dying to know who Miss Sissy's man was, but for now, all she wanted was the straight dope about her relationship with Dink.

Miss Sissy, she noticed, was as calm as a cucumber, much more so than Dink was when he told his side of the story. Nadine decided she was going to accept what she told her for now, but she wasn't totally convinced she was telling the truth. Not yet, anyway.

A voice deep inside of her was telling her something was not quite right with this entire situation. She knew Miss Sissy, and she knew women like her, because she used to be one. She recalled how she went after the evangelist, Preacher Gene, that night, and it shamed her now. She still felt Miss Sissy had designs on Dink, though. There was no way to prove it, however, so she figured until some concrete evidence presented itself, she'd leave it alone for the time being.

Nadine knew how to act about as well as Miss Sissy when she had to, and this was one of those times. She decided to play the naïve, ignorant, country girl and be all-forgiving, so she held out her arms to Miss Sissy.

"Will you give me a hug?" she asked, sounding sweet as honey. "Miss Sissy, if I've offended you, I'm sorry. You have been so sweet and good to us. I don't want this to be a thorn between us in our friendship. We all think the world of you, and you've made us all look so pretty today."

Miss Sissy held her in a big bear hug for several moments.

"Darling, darling," Miss Sissy said, speaking in that low baby talk she could turn on like a light switch. "Don't let this concern you one iota. I've already forgotten it. You girls are such a blessing to me, but there's something I want you to do."

"Sure, anything," Nadine said.

"Don't ask Wanda Faye about this right now, because I don't want to spoil her wedding day, but I want her to keep an eye on Lollie for me. She's had some mighty bad looking bruises on her arms and legs, even one time up around her neck and ear. I asked her about it, and she told me she'd been jogging early in the mornings and had fallen down a couple of times. Miss Sissy's been around a long time, and I'm suspicious of that little druggist she's going with up in Valdosta. I hope I don't find that Mr. Fast Ass is putting his hands on my niece. If he is, there'll be hell to pay."

Nadine's ears perked up, and all talk about Wanda Faye, Dink and Miss Sissy's possible indiscretions were now overshadowed with more juicy gossip.

"Miss Sissy, do you reckon he's beating her like them programs talk about on television?" Nadine asked. "Miss Margot was talking about it the other day when me and Wanda Faye was watching her show."

"I'm not sure," Miss Sissy said. "I know your sister has been down the road of physical abuse, and I traveled down that road just a short trip in my younger days, but nobody should be whipping and beating on another person, especially in the name of love."

"Well, me, Wanda Faye and Destini will keep our eyes and ears opened, and we'll help you. If that man is beatin' on Lollie, we'll find out."

Miss Sissy kissed Nadine on the cheek and took her hand.

"I knew I could depend on you, sugar," she said. "Now let's go get some of that delicious wedding cake. I promised Mr. Yuk, Tang and Lee that I'd bring them back some. I know they'll enjoy it."

Chapter 33

Dink pulled Wanda Faye aside for a few moments during a lull in the excitement of the wedding reception and told her he had one last surprise for his new wife.

"You know how you've always talked about wanting to go to one of them big country music concerts over in Pittstown?" he asked her.

"You mean at the big music park on the other side of the river? The one we could never, ever afford to go to?"

"Yeah, that one," he said with a wide grin. "Well, I talked with the man who owns the place, Mr. Herbert Huxby, and he's gonna let us use one of their big log cabins for two nights. He said it's the one they reserve for newlyweds."

"Oh, my God! Are you serious?"

"Yes, ma'am, and this cabin hangs right over top of the Suwannee River. He said the view is spectacular. They're also having a concert out on the lawn tonight that he said we'd really like."

"You mean we're going there tonight?" Wanda Faye asked, completely dumbfounded. "But I thought we agreed to stay at the camp lodge since Mr. Hamp was givin' it to us as a weddin' gift."

"Well, honey, it's up to you. We can go either or," Dink said. "Mr. Huxby said he ain't chargin' me a dime for the cabin, though, since I do such a good job maintaining all them vehicles they use out there at the park, including all the golf carts. When he heard I was gettin' married, he kinda insisted."

Just then, Mr. Hamp came up behind them.

"You two lovebirds take Mr. Huxby up on that offer," he said to them. "You can come stay at my lodge anytime y'all want, but an opportunity like this don't come up all that often. Go on and enjoy yourselves."

"Oh, thank you, Mr. Hamp," Wanda Faye said and she hugged him around the neck before turning back toward Dink. "Well, whatcha waitin' for, Mr. Drayfuss Lowell? Let's get this show on the road!"

"You got it, Mrs. Wanda Faye Lowell!" Dink said, and the two shared a long, passionate kiss.

As the reception was winding down, Wanda Faye decided it was time to get out of her wedding suit and change into something more comfortable for their trip to the music park.

When she emerged from the ladies room a few minutes later, she had on a simple camel-colored corduroy pants ensemble with a lacy print blouse. Everybody commented how pretty she looked. Meanwhile, all Dink did was take off his jacket and tie, and pull his shirt out from his slacks.

Before the newlyweds left the fellowship hall to begin their journey as husband and wife, Wanda Faye visited with Mr. Hamp for a bit. He was sitting by himself at a table in the back of the hall. She sat down next to him and thanked him again for everything, including the amazing rehearsal dinner, the new freezer, and all the meat he had stocked inside. In his usual self-effacing manner, he told her to think nothing of it.

Just then, Bunnye came running over to him and climbed up in his lap. From the time she was a toddler, she'd always run to him, sit in his lap, and he'd feed her cookies, candy, or whatever he happened to have in his hand at the time. This time, it was wedding cake.

As he offered a forkful to Bunnye, Wanda Faye smiled. Then, as if stricken by a bolt of lightning, something popped into her mind. Something she had never dared think about before. As quickly as the thought appeared in her head, she banished it.

"No, that ain't right," she thought, as the smile left her face.

It was one of those strange, haunting thoughts, like a goblin or a specter. It made a sudden appearance and then it was gone. In this instance, however, the memory of it stayed with her longer than it should have. She dared not verbalize it, ever, and decided to put it in the back vault of her brain.

After all, this was her wedding day, a day of happiness and joy. There was no need for any unpleasant thoughts today.

A few minutes later, as Wanda Faye hugged and kissed her children goodbye, and told them to mind Aunt Nadine and Aunt Destini, she realized this would be the longest amount of time she'd ever been away from her kids. It would only be two nights and three days, but it seemed almost sinful.

"Wanda Faye, are you ready to go?" Dink asked her.

"Ready as I'll ever be," she said. "Oops! Almost forgot! There's one more thing I gotta do!"

Wanda Faye grabbed one of the bridesmaid's nosegays off a nearby table to use for a bouquet, since she was wearing her orchid as a corsage on her going away suit. Destini, whether she intended to or not, caught the bridal bouquet, which set her up for lots of playful, taunting remarks, which she seemed to be enjoying.

Out in front of the fellowship hall was Dink's pickup, all decorated with shaving cream and shoe polish, as well as soup cans and old boots that would be dragging behind them until the roadway got the better of them.

Moments later, Wanda Faye and Dink were inside the truck. The newlyweds were smiling and waving to the crowd that was gathered on the lawn as they pulled away, leaving a cloud of dust behind them.

On the way to the music park, Wanda Faye's thoughts drifted back to the last Margot Smith show she had watched. Margot was talking about new beginnings and how new beginnings often brought joy, but a little sadness, too.

She was proud to be Dink's wife, and she was proud to be starting a new life with him, but she was sad about leaving her children behind. Then, there was still that nagging, aching pain at the center of her heart.

"Make the world go away and get it off my shoulders," she thought wistfully to herself. "Say the things you used to say, and make the world go away."

Chapter 34

It was about four o'clock in the afternoon when Dink and Wanda Faye arrived at Pittstown Country Music Park. Right out front by the entrance was a huge banner that read, "Welcome Mr. and Mrs. Drayfuss Lowell! Congratulations on your wedding!"

The excited couple received a royal escort to their honeymoon cabin by a parade of folks, mostly visiting campers who were in town for the big concert that night, in brightly decorated golf carts. They were all tossing flower petals along the sandy road that led to the log cabin, as hundreds of bystanders along the narrow roadway shouted cheers to them as they passed by.

Once inside the cabin, the first thing that caught Wanda Faye's eye was a huge arrangement of colorful flowers on the dining room table. Alongside it was a basket of fresh fruit and lying on the table was a card with a picture of Dink and Wanda Faye on the front.

Inside, it read, "We love you and appreciate

you. Congratulations, Herbert Huxby and the entire staff at Pittstown Country Music Park."

Meanwhile, Dink had gone over to the refrigerator to retrieve a bottle of champagne. After he popped the cork, he poured them both a glass, making use of the two crystal flutes that were sitting on the kitchen counter.

Wanda Faye spotted a large platter of cookies, cakes and pastries that were sitting on the other side of the counter.

"These look like Salvation Sweets, don't they, Dink?" she asked her husband.

"They are," he said, with a big grin on his face. "Your mama's Bible Drill team helped make them and they brought the platter over here early this morning."

"Oh, my word, Dink! You mean mama and all them knew about this?! And they didn't tell me?"

"Well, 'course they all knew," Dink said, laughing, as he held her in his arms.

"You sly, little devil, you," she said, and she planted a wet, sloppy kiss on his lips.

"Here's to us, honey," Dink said, as he handed Wanda Faye her glass of champagne. "May we live in the holiest of matrimony for the rest of our lives."

"Here, here!" she shouted.

After entwining their arms together, the two of them downed the divine liquid in one huge swallow.

It was then that Wanda Faye happened to spot another familiar item sitting on the counter. Right beside the coffeemaker was an entire box of the individually packaged Jamaican Coffee that Destini had received from her Camp EZ guest. Taped to the box was a note from Destini and Nadine. Wanda Faye read it out loud.

"Don't stay up too late tonight. Remember, honey, if you can't be good, be good at it."

Both of them had a good laugh.

"Them two's crazy as sprayed roaches," Dink said.

"That's for sure," Wanda Faye said, and then she set out to explore the rest of the cabin.

It was a beautiful structure, set high above the river with a birds-eye view of the big outdoor music stage. Dink told her it was used primarily to entertain VIP's who came to the concerts.

This weekend's concert was a three-day country music and bluegrass extravaganza with some of the best known regional musical talent to ever hit the stage.

After the two of them changed into jeans, country-styled, long-sleeved shirts and matching cowboy hats, they went outside and hopped into the golf cart that Mr. Huxby had so graciously let them use free of charge.

When they arrived at the outdoor stage, the lead male vocalist of the band abruptly stopped singing, as the music continued softly behind him.

"Ladies and gentlemen, we have a couple of newlyweds with us tonight," he said. "Mr. Huxby, the owner of the park, has offered free champagne for everyone here tonight. So, let's raise our glasses and drink a toast to Dink and Wanda Faye Lowell. Congratulations on your wedding day!" he shouted.

There was thunderous applause from the crowd and numerous shouts of congratulations. Many, including Mr. Huxby, even went over and hugged Dink and Wanda Faye. It seemed Dink had a lot of friends at the music park, since he worked on so much of their equipment. Wanda Faye was taken aback at the outpouring of love they received from everyone.

Dink had told Wanda Faye earlier that Mr. Huxby worked hard to bring quality entertainment to the region. He said he was conscientious and had a good sense of humor. Even though Wanda Faye was now a married woman, she had to admit he was a good looking man and she told Dink so.

"That's why his lady friend, Miss Susie, keeps him on such a tight leash," Dink told her.

Wanda Faye and Dink had front row seats to watch the rest of the concert. When the first act finished their set, folks in the audience began shouting, "Kiss the Bride!"

Dink, not wanting to disappoint any of his

friends, asked his blushing bride to stand up beside him. Then, he bent her over and, as if they were the stars of a Broadway theatrical production, he put his lips to hers and engaged her in a long, drawn out, sloppy, wet kiss that nearly brought the house down with reverberating applause and shouts of, “More! More!”

By seven o’clock that evening, both Wanda Faye and Dink realized they were starving, so they went over to the restaurant and munched on a basket of hot buffalo wings, and a large side of French fries.

When they went back to the music stage, an Elvis impersonator had just come up to begin his set.

“Good evening ladies and gentlemen!” he shouted. “My name is Elvis... oops, I mean Johnny McCool Presley! Oh, whatever... y’all know who I am!” he added, and the crowd laughed and clapped as he took several bows.

Wanda Faye and Dink were just about to sit down in their reserved seats when Johnny McCool summoned them up onstage.

“Dink and Wanda Faye, our newlywed guests of honor, come on out on the dance floor!” he shouted.

As Johnny McCool broke into Elvis Presley’s hit, “Love me Tender”, Wanda Faye looked deep into Dink’s eyes and then kissed him sweetly on the lips.

For the first time in many years, a feeling of comfort swept over her, as if, from now on, everything was going to be all right. As he held her in his arms and slow-danced with her, she felt loved and secure. It was an awesome feeling.

The next song was "Jailhouse Rock" and Johnny McCool invited the audience to join Wanda Faye and Dink on the dance floor.

She and Dink were laughing and kissing each other as they danced together when Mr. Huxby and his lady friend, Miss Susie, broke in on them to dance with the bride and the groom.

The rest of the evening was simply magical, Wanda Faye thought, just as the entire day had been. She and Dink never spent a cent all night on food and drink, either.

Even when they tried to pay their bill at the restaurant, the old, salty bartender, Tom, who had worked at the park since they opened more than twenty years ago, wouldn't take a dime from Dink. Not even a tip.

All he said to them was, "No charge, lovebirds. May all your roads be smooth ones, and all your troubles be few. From the Pittstown Country Music Park, we all love you."

Wanda Faye had reached across the bar and kissed him on the cheek.

"You're a sweetheart," she told him.

"You keep that to yourself," he said and he smiled wide at the two of them.

As the evening wound down and the crowd began to disperse, Dink grabbed Wanda Faye's hand and said, "The night's not over yet."

As if right on cue, a horse-drawn buggy pulled up beside them and the driver, Mr. Huxby himself, invited the two to step inside for a special moonlight ride through the park. It was more magical than anything Wanda Faye could have dreamt up in her wildest dreams.

When Mr. Huxby dropped them off at their cabin about thirty minutes later, Wanda Faye noticed someone had brought their golf cart back and parked it right by the front steps for them to use for the rest of their stay at the park.

That night, as they lie wrapped in each other's arms, staring out the window at the big, yellow moon, Wanda Faye drifted off into a deep, peaceful sleep, thanking God for all her many blessings.

Chapter 35

The next two days were happy ones for the newly married couple, which included another wonderful surprise for both of them. Their final hours at the music park blurred together, as they experienced plenty of laughter, lots of lovemaking, music, walking under the stars, and even a boat ride up and down the Suwannee River.

On their last day at the park, as they were getting everything packed up to head back home, Sheriff Lewis called Dink on his cell phone with some uplifting news. He informed Dink that government agents agreed to give him and Wanda Faye a fifty-thousand dollar reward for turning in the nearly one million dollars that Chester had taken in from his illegal drug dealing.

Every one of Chester's illegal activities, as well as all the bitter memories etched in Wanda Faye's mind from her life with him in Ludowici, she thought, made her truly deserving of the reward money. It was money that would be well spent to help her, Dink and the children embark on a brand new life together as husband, wife and family.

A few days after they made it back to Seraph Springs, a Cuban gentleman from Miami, by the name of Justo Guillermo Fernandez called Dink. Fernandez owned a trucking company that transported fruits and vegetables from South Miami to points north.

One of the major transfer sites for the company was just north of Atlanta, Georgia. Mr. Fernandez told Dink that, while he had plenty of drivers to make long hauls, he was in need of independent operators to truck goods to the transfer site in Georgia. When he told Dink how much he could make within a year's time, he nearly dropped the phone. It was more than three times what he was making as a mechanic.

Dink already had his CDL license, so he was qualified to drive 18-wheelers. It was something he acquired a number of years ago when a special course was offered over in Pittstown.

He was one of the best students in the class, and the instructor tried, at that time, to get him to drive for a company he knew in Jacksonville, but Dink declined, since it meant living in Jacksonville, which he had no desire to do.

Mr. Fernandez also told Dink that if he owned his own rig, his schedule would be more flexible, and he would guarantee his runs would be finished by Friday afternoon, so he could have weekends at home. He told Dink to think about it and give him a call back within the week.

After much discussion between Dink and Wanda Faye, they agreed that the fifty grand reward money they just received would serve as a major down payment on a brand new 18-wheeler.

"It will be a good investment for us," Wanda Faye told Dink.

They debated the pros and cons all week long. Since Wanda Faye was finishing up nursing school in the next few months, she told Dink that the time they could spend together on weekends would be quality time for the entire family.

Of course, Wanda Faye did have one ulterior motive. With Dink on the road all week, he'd be far away from any temptation that might come from Betty's Beauty Box, a.k.a. Miss Sissy's House of Horrors that Nadine had dubbed it just the other day.

Chapter 36

Chester Easley's confession

Up in Ludowici, the House of Prayer was in the midst of their fifth night of a one-week revival service. The Spirit of God was moving at the House of Prayer, and many of the members knew that Brother Chester Easley's honest, open and emotional testimony during the service was being used as an instrument of the Holy Spirit to bring people to Jesus.

Each night, Chester would sing a solo and then give a moving testimony. Tonight he was singing a beautiful gospel song written by a couple from Turpricone, Florida.

The congregation joined in for the chorus, which resounded throughout the little sanctuary.

"I can't even walk without you holding my hand.

The mountain's too high and the valley's too wide.

Down on my knees is where I learned to

stand.

Lord, I can't even walk without you holding my hand."

As the chorus ended, the shouts of "Hallelujah" and "Amen" could be heard throughout the small cinder block church, as well as halfway down the block.

"Praise the Lord for that song and for the Brother and Sister in Turpricone, Florida, who wrote it," Chester told the crowd. "Tonight, my beloved, I want to tell you a story. It's a story about a man who turned his back on the Lord and tried to make it on his own. This young man traveled down a road that led him to evil dens of drugs, and into places where those drugs were made."

"Amen, brother!" someone shouted from the back of the church.

"This young man thought money would buy happiness," Chester continued. "He made millions of dollars selling dope that harmed young people and others all over this nation. This man had a loving wife and children, and he treated his wife badly. He beat her, he abused her, and he did all manner of unspeakable things to her."

Chester's eyes filled with tears, as they had done each and every time he told his story.

"During all this time, this man told his wife how much he loved her," Chester said, looking out across all the faces staring back at him. "He played the bass guitar right here in this church each Sunday, and he told the Lord, I love you, but he wasn't serving the Lord and he wasn't loving anyone but himself."

The "Amen's" were coming at him now in rapid fire succession, one after the next, as he spoke.

"This young man was arrested, tried, and sent to prison for his wrongdoing," Chester went on. "In his prison cell, he was brutally abused, sexually abused, and he lived in constant fear. There were many days he felt he had been deserted, that God had forgotten about him. Just when he was about to lose all hope, he received a letter from an elderly lady here in this church. Sister Merle, stand up, honey. This little saint of God sent me a letter while I was in prison."

Chester pulled the letter out from his Bible and read it aloud.

"Dear Chester, I've known you since you were born. I just want you to know I love you and, more importantly, Jesus loves you. Remember, darling, Jesus loves you."

"Week after week, the same letter came in the mail," Chester continued. "There were other letters that came, but there was never a letter that meant more to me than that one, because through that letter, the Lord spoke to me, and I knew I was not forgotten. Praise the Lord, I was not forgotten. Tonight, I am a living testimony that Jesus is able to deliver you from the depths of despair. He delivered the Hebrew children from the fiery furnace, and he delivered Daniel from the Lion's den. He delivered God's chosen people out from the bondage of Egypt. He is able to deliver you from any sin, any wrong, anything you've done. God takes that bill on which is written all those sins, all those bad things, and he stamps in His blood, paid in full."

By the time Chester finished his testimony, there was shouting and glorifying God throughout the sanctuary. Many came to the altar and received salvation. Still others came forward and re-dedicated their lives to the Lord.

That night after the revival meeting, Chester slept the whole night through. For the first time in a long, long time, he didn't dream about Daddy, and he didn't hear Daddy's voice speaking all those vile words to him.

Instead, he dreamed about a building, a safe place, and a peaceful place that was attached to the House of Prayer. It was a shelter for those who needed a place to stay, until they could move on and have a home of their own.

Chester saw a sign in the dream. On it was written, "Jesus is the answer." Then, he heard a choir singing, "Jesus is the answer for the world today."

When he awakened the next morning, he knew what he had to do. He must make certain the shelter became a reality. He had a mission.

He had lost a lot over the years, but now he was going to be a builder... a builder of hope for the lost and the forlorn.

He recalled an old song that was sung at the House of Prayer when he was a child. As he sat in his kitchen sipping his morning coffee, the song reverberated through his mind.

"I'm working on a building,
I'm working on a building,
I'm working on a building for my Lord, for my Lord.
It's a Holy Ghost building,
It's a Holy Ghost building.
It's a Holy Ghost building for my Lord, for my Lord."

Just like the lyrics of the old song, Chester would now be "working on a building." There would be no more Daddy, no more fear, and no more regrets. He meant to make the Lord proud. He was going to serve him and others.

Secretly, he prayed each night that the Lord would allow him to see his children one day soon, and on that day, his children would be proud of him. Maybe then, Wanda Faye would give him another chance.

He knew it was a lot to ask the Lord after all the sins he had committed, but he prayed the same prayer night after night, and he didn't let up. He knew God's timetable was not his. While in prison, he had learned the virtue of patience. He thought about a scripture, and then took a pen to paper. He wrote:

"They who wait upon the Lord shall renew their strength. They shall rise up on wings like eagles. They shall run and not be weary. They shall walk and not faint. Teach me Lord to wait."

About the author

White Springs native Johnny Bullard was born in a place where two cities and two counties interconnect on the banks of the historic Suwannee River. His family roots run about seven generations deep into the sandy soil of north central Florida, a place he dearly loves and where his entire life has been spent as an educator, public servant, musical performer and writer.

Born into a family of prolific storytellers, Bullard absorbed all the tales that were told aloud, as well as the ones whispered quietly inside screened porches and around the dining room table when family and close friends gathered together.

Bullard's grasp of the culture and life of this region is expressed by one who has not only lived it, but who loves it and is a part of it. He offers a humorous, poignant and honest voice of a South that is still colorful, vibrant, rich and real. Bullard is as much a part of the region as the historic Suwannee River, immortalized by Stephen C. Foster in the unforgettable tune, "Old Folks at Home".

An old turpentine distillery at the Eight Mile Still on the Woodpecker Route north of White Springs is where Bullard calls home. He boasts four college degrees from Valdosta State University in Georgia, including a B.A. in English. He also did post graduate work at Florida State University in Tallahassee, Florida, and was privileged to be selected to attend the prestigious Harvard Principal's Center at Harvard University in Cambridge, Massachusetts in 1993.

Bullard writes a weekly column, "Around the Banks of the Suwannee", which is published in the *Jasper News* and *Suwannee Democrat* newspapers. He has also written magazine articles for several well known publications including *Forum*, a quarterly publication of the Florida Humanities Council.

His weekly newspaper column always ends with his signature message to all his readers, friends and relatives throughout the region. He writes, "From the Eight Mile Still on the Woodpecker Route north of White Springs, I wish you all a day filled with joy, peace, and above all, lots of love and laughter."

❧❧❧❧❧

Editor's note:

If you enjoyed reading "Nightshade", then you will most definitely enjoy the second half of this thrilling duology, which is due out in the very near future, entitled "Secrets".

Master storyteller Johnny Bullard will keep you enthralled with the continuing saga of life in Seraph Springs where the Deep South meets the Suwannee River.

Will Wanda Faye and Dink's marriage endure the test of time, or will convicted felon Chester Easley and his troubled past intrude upon his ex wife's wedded bliss? Will Destini's long-buried secret ever come out into the open? What other secrets might be revealed that could potentially destroy people's lives?

Sometimes, if we're lucky, secrets can bring joy and happiness. Other times, we're not so lucky. Find out the answers to all your probing questions when "Secrets" hits the streets in 2016.

Joyce Marie Taylor
Editor

❧❧❧❧❧

78130523R00183

Made in the USA
Columbia, SC
11 October 2017